Bigot Hall

STEVE AYLETT was born in 1967. He works as a belching consultant and has the ability to become a silhouette at will. 1994 saw the publication of his book *The Crime Studio*, a work widely regarded as a cry for help.

Bigot Hall

A Gothic Childhood

Steve Aylett

Serif
London

First published 1995 by
Serif
47 Strahan Road
London E3 5DA

British Library Cataloguing-in-Publication Data.
A catalogue record for this book
is available from the British Library.

Library of Congress Cataloging in Publication Data.
A catalog record for this book
is available from the Library of Congress.

ISBN 1 897959 20 6

For Myra

Photoset in North Wales by
Derek Doyle and Associates, Mold, Clwyd
Printed and bound in Great Britain by
Biddles of Guildford

'On the contrary.'

Henrik Ibsen's dying words, upon hearing his wife remark that he was looking better

Contents

BANISHMENT

Even in the slaughterhouse of boyhood I was dimly aware that I should have some jolly, wink-eyed uncle or gramp with whom to share private jokes and hatch terrorist outrages against the state. But all I recall is Uncle Snapper, who liked to go shooting in the woods and had a theory about squirrels. 'They always run round the other side of the tree from where I am,' he declared one evening, at which I in my innocence said I wasn't surprised seeing as he went into the woods for the exclusive purpose of killing anything larger than his brain.

At this Uncle Snapper stood in a shuddering, grill-mouthed rage.

'Dad!' I shouted down the hallway. 'Uncle Snap's changing colour!'

'Right you are,' called Father from his study, but did not emerge to look. Snapper convulsed his stiffened arms.

'Dad!' I shouted down the hallway. 'It's a seizure — grand mal or I'm a rat!'

'Offer him water,' called Father, preoccupied. He was by nature so calm he once sketched an oncoming bullet train before stepping unhurriedly aside. This despite his supposed descent from an Irish berserker famous for having beaten off the rigid head of a goat. It was Snap who seemed determined to inherit the legend's ancient umbrage and who wasted no time in breaking a bull's nose with his left fist. But it was a cause for the odd explosive guffaw that this had been the outer and extreme extent of his effect upon the animal kingdom.

Snapper bellowed suddenly, grabbed my neck and shook me like a bladder on a stick. Apparently the blur of my mouth and eyes resembled the slot and gauge of a parking meter. 'You'll help me kill those woodland rascals, laughing boy,' he snarled, jowls quivering, 'or so help me I'll —'

The following day, Uncle Snapper stood in the leaf-blown forest with a sawn-off 20-bore and a pair of strange, inflatable dungarees. I stood by cheerlessly as he outlined the stalking plan in a guarded, barely articulate whisper. 'An animal,' he stated, 'can only be in one place at a time.'

'One *area*,' said I, thinking of the very long tail of the Portuguese man-of-war. Those beauties are only filled with gas, but by god they can sting a man.

Snapper was furious, pounding me on the chops in time with his heartrate. He explained that if he and I stood on opposite sides of the tree, a trunkbound squirrel would have nowhere to hide. This is the sort of shite I had to listen to when I was a boy.

We set about executing Snapper's plan — ofcourse the chosen squirrel couldn't care less and clung flat to my side of the trunk, regarding me with a beady eye. 'What's it doing?' shouted Snapper.

'Hanging there, Uncle. And staring at me as if awaiting some grand finale.'

'I'll give it a finale,' Snapper choked, and told me to scare it into his sights. The most scary thing I could think of was the fact that unstable statesmen are only deemed insane retrospectively. As Eisenhower said, 'Things are more like they are now than they ever were before' — if those aren't the words of a florid psychopath I'm all ears. Anyway I discussed migraine humour and other things which interested me at the time. But the squirrel just looked me in the face with all the self-possessed assurance of an elderly barber. Initially I couldn't assess how Snapper was reacting due to the interposing tree — then there was an almighty blast and a scatter of lead which almost brought my life of abysmal horseplay to an end. He thundered into view, his bonce as red as a brick. 'By god you've done it now!' he roared, and I was already running as fast as my arms and legs could take me.

'Dad!' I yelled, crashing into the study, 'Uncle Snap's having a funny turn — from failing to shoot even one mammal!'

'Another fruitless siege,' said Father in his deep voice, and looked pensively through the window at the largest tree. He turned from his drawingboard, on which was set a convoluted architectural plan, and lay a hand on my head. 'Your uncle,' he remarked, 'is a man for whom thought is an hourly ceremony.'

A stranger to joy, I had eked out my only endorphin by feeding it through a mangle. Yet such a callow boy was I that I sought to dissolve Snapper's woe by nailing a multitude of soft, polychrome effigies to the forestation. Some of these did not even represent squirrels but toads, and every one was made of brushed corduroy and wool. However, as I hammered them up in the dark I felt they could pass as almost anything. And best of all, not only were there dozens of the brutes but they'd never move a muscle. 'No running round the other side for *this* lot,' said I proudly, driving the final nail.

But in the stark light of dawn Snapper stared in baffled indignation at a forest hung with boggle-eyed, multicoloured perversions of nature, as out of place as balloons in a hearse. No true animal was this densely packed with dried beans. Positioned near the tree-base, they were clearly the work of a small and immoral child.

Snap, who took a poor view of the fact that I had ever been born, entered my room in a broth of anger. I looked up from a join-the-dot picture of Trotsky's abrupt demise. Where Snap's mouth should have been was merely a blinding explosion of profanity. 'Beanbag toads, is it?' he added, and began belting me with a violence over which I will draw a discrete veil.

That afternoon, I chanced upon a dead ladybird by the hot-house, and hurried to the drawing room. 'Here's something you can kill, Snapper,' I said, swanning up with a matchbox. Pushing out the tray, I showed him the contents while tilting the box imperceptibly from side to side, so that the dead ladybird rolled apparently of its own accord.

'A ladybird,' stated Snapper, flushing purple. 'And dead.'

'Not dead,' I countered with a nervous laugh. 'Not dead Uncle, rolling — rolling for pleasure.'

'Rolling for pleasure eh,' muttered Snapper, his eyes like the gun-slits of a tank. 'Do you expect me to believe this crudely-fashioned tale?'

'Well don't be offended Uncle, but I don't prance through

life planning my every move in anticipation of what *you*'ll subsequently believe.'

I sniggered good-humouredly.

Uncle Snapper strove visibly to contain his impulses and gestured at the bug. 'What d'you think *this* microscopic trophy would look like on a wallmount?'

'A zit,' I replied.

'Oh Snapper,' said Adrienne, my girlfriend and sister, as the family and lodgers sat identifying the evening meal. I was by now festooned with bandages. 'You must make a sincere effort to keep your more demented opinions to yourself.'

'I *beg* your pardon?'

Adrienne repeated her statement, staring at him levelly. But Uncle Snapper believed he could release his prejudices only by expressing them, and would believe this until he was buried in worms and clay.

In a final attempt to relieve his torment, I tempted a squirrel to the woodside shed and patiently taught it to play dead at the sound of a gunshot. But hearing shots and my cry of 'Die!', passing villagers feared the worst and twenty-seven of them alerted the authorities. I had to relate my elaborate plans to the local constabulary who, despite the stark simplicity of my account, demanded a demonstration. I was fast learning that official bodies communicate by synchronised backwardness. Snapper shot Camille — as I had come to know the animal — stone dead. For this Snap was lauded by the constabulary and was slapped on the back so often his spine appeared through the pulp. Snap's delighted surprise was as nothing to my shock on finding that Camille wasn't play-acting and that I was being detained for mayhem and for weaving a windtorn web of lies to the law.

'Dad!' I shouted.

Back at the Hall, Father explained his plans to Snapper
— a large, groaning treehouse rigged into the tallest garden
oak. It was understood that Snapper would not only live
there but become a figure of fear and superstition to the
village children. This could easily be arranged — it had
happened to Nanny Jack without any arrangements being
necessary.

'But that child attempted every trick in the book,'
Snapper complained, sobbing like a bullring clown, 'to stop
me killing one of them bushy vermin.'

'Silence, brother. Did I, too, not make every effort when
we were the boy's age? Don't you need ammo and
medication from the village?' Father fixed him with a stern
look. 'And wasn't he the one made it possible for you to
shoot something at long last?'

Snapper went before the cops and confessed to
everything, including several genuine and horrific crimes of
which none of us had been previously aware. He became a
marked man, and we finally found him digging up fossil
spuds in a rain-ripped field, barely human for the mud and
darkness.

At breakfast it was decided that we could not harbour
Snapper at the Hall. Father built the treehouse and Snapper
moved in with his armoury, descending only for meals and
an occasional whirling, snorting rampage of destruction.

As we buried Camille, Adrienne sang mournfully and
dark-eyed in the rain:

> Tortoises are vacuum-sealed
> And breaking down is sickly,
> But your bones are all internal
> So you'll rot more quickly.

The darkness was eating at her like a vacuum at a matchflame. The rain fell like Hiroshima dust. She kissed a rose and lay it on the burial mound. I wanted to remove her skulltop and slather my tongue through her brainfolds. Even in grief there is diversity.

DOCUMENT

Chairman Mao said 'My enemy's enemy is my friend.' The friends he made this way were inevitably lost by the corresponding principle that 'My friend's friend is my enemy.' The fractal shifts generated by the two principles kept Mao's relationships in a swirl-state of constant and luridly violent flux. I could draw parallels between this and the environment of my youth which would make your nostrils flare.

The Hall was a fertile chaos of bellowing sociopaths, arc-welding nuns and sudden combat. Rarely was anything done without a scream. My earliest memory is of Snap throwing a lobster into a bonfire and cursing as the creature exploded. I'm the first to admit the violence lacked texture but it was leavened with a quality of ferocious disregard. Ask to use the phone and you'd be met with a dead stare. We once detained a postman for eight months by locking him in the cellar and telling him he knew why. I live in amazement that I did not mature to stagger bearded in the streets, baying evangelically at strangers. Childhood was a losing battle to remain ignorant in the face of pulse-browed maniacs, shrieking chimps, arrogant liars, knife-fights, angry swans, a grandmother you'd swerve to hit and a spaniel whom everyone mysteriously asserted was 'more than a mere dog'. I once dredged an old, streaming skull from the lake and figured a thing of that size and shape would effortlessly plug the fossil gap. I cut it in half with a hacksaw and found there was no brain cavity — only recurring skulls, one inside another like the layers of an onion. But it just turned out to be some aunt or other.

I had always been troubled that my ancestors did not go back in sequence — a family tree hung in the boiler room seemed to represent the ricochet path of a bullet. I took this to Professor Leap, who was bashing a guppy against a drystone wall. 'Not in sequence, you say?' He frowned at the diagram. 'You're at the top,' he said. 'It's simply drawn upside down.' But Adrienne, who was only four years my senior, was near the middle, Father was at the base, Nan was near the top and Professor Leap himself — a lodger unrelated to the family — appeared to be the mother of them all.

Billy Verlag, a barrel-like boy from the village, said the chart was an origami sheet with fold-guides, and twisted it into the shape of a piece of trash. He looked up at me with a ruddy face, a nose which contained his brain and a smile which contained my fist.

'An astronomical starmap, perhaps?' stated Father, raising his eyebrows.

'What kind of simple-minded lout of an astronomer would name a star *Leap* for god's sake, or *Jack*?'

'Your great grandfather was just such a man — the telescope in your sister's sanctuary belonged to him.' And he pointed at the wall. 'There is a daguerreotype of that venerable gentleman strangling what I can only describe as a hen.'

The wall was, in fact, bare.

I showed Adrienne the document. 'Text and line,' she said. 'Quite clearly it's a work of conceptual art.'

'What does that mean?'

'That you can throw it away.'

'Take a butcher's at this, Verger,' I said to the Verger, who was busy walloping a village dog about the muzzle.

'What is it, boy?' he roared, straightening up. 'By god you've arrogance to burn!'

'Found this in the steam room,' I said, giving him the chart.

Viewing it, his eyes opened wide, then seemed to seal over with disdain. He regarded me through a visor of disapproval. 'Oh what a tangled web we weave,' he rumbled.

'But you say that even if I'm just mowing the lawn,' I complained. 'What does it *represent*, Verger?'

'What does it represent he says. Without a doubt and despite all I have tried to teach you, this here is a chart of who owes who money.'

'Money?' I said, frowning. 'So I can afford a caulking hammer at long bloody last.'

'The debt proceeds downward. You are at the top.' He fixed me with a baleful eye. 'And always will be.'

Poor Mr Cannon the lodger regarded the paper with a lively interest. 'This is a floorplan, laughing boy, showing the relative positioning of our dungeons in the scorching deeps of hell. You and I will be able to yell abominations at eachother across the skull-littered hallway, our faces tear-rashed and demented. One thing at least to look forward to,' he grinned.

I was getting desperate. In two rare moments of lucidity Uncle Burst stared at the paper and whispered the word 'hex' and then, late the following day, 'evil spirits'.

Nanny Jack was propped like a dummy in the kitchen.

'What do you make of this, old woman?' I said, slapping the sheet onto the table before her.

Nanny Jack was unresponsive.

'The paper, Nan!' I shouted, stabbing a finger at the chart. 'What does it say to you?' Nan's disquieting immobility continued unabated. 'For god's sake, Nan, give me some good news!' I bellowed into her ear. 'Am I talking to my*self*?' And I collapsed into wracking sobs, hiding my face and ears against the tabletop.

It was during one of the household's attempts to bury Nan — a tradition in which Uncle Snapper played a leading role while I was considered too young to participate — that I sat poring over the chart again. By now the document had taken on the enigmatic monumentalism of ancient scripture. It occurred to me that the only name missing was Snapper's, and with time to spare before his return, I climbed into the creaking treehouse. Adjusting to the rocking of the floor and the ebb and flow of clattering furniture, I plucked a little book from a passing table. It was Snapper's diary, a marker at the latest entry:

Today, laughing boy taunts me. But I do not give up! There I am in the living room when in he comes, parping on a bugle. Strutting like a feudal lord and talking about verte-brae as if they were the main event. Is this the behaviour of a respectful child? Or that of a glad and devious boy? You could lay track on his insolence. But the day will come when everyone will know me as I am. They'll be stamping my

*features onto coins the size of manhole covers. God grant
me the strength to do what's necessary.*

With ballooning apprehension, I surveyed the poster of
the *Desiderata* which Snap used for target practice. A corner
was bent over showing the flap of something underneath. I
yanked out a pin and the *Desiderata* scrolled upward like a
rollerblind, revealing a giant version of the famous name
chart. A hit-list, and a thorough one. Next to my name were
the words 'gun, bomb or poison'. The others, too, had been
assigned a method: 'Leap — knife; Burst — ligature; Jack
— axe; the Verger — harpoon bolt' and so on. My world
turned inside-out like an umbrella. Where would I be safe?
I had run away to the circus once but was deemed 'too
rough with the lions'.

As I clambered down the rope-ladder the crew were
arriving back at the Hall. Snapper tramped through the
chill air, the whole household trailing after. Sad faces all
round — the funeral had not succeeded. 'Run for cover you
morons,' I yelled, 'Snapper's a homicidal maniac. We're
headed full-tilt for a bloodbath!' Everyone stopped, staring
at me as though at a mildly irritating street performer.
'Look out,' I said, 'he'll murder the bloody lot of you —
and me most of all! Mercy, Snapper — the devil is boring
and I'm scared to die! Could you harm a little boy?'
Blowing my nose on a crow, I shed tears which I would later
defensively dismiss as auxiliary pieces of brain.

It was an entire month of sniggers and gibes before I tore
the Christmas wrapping from a gun, a bomb and a bottle of
arsenic. 'Couldn't decide,' said Snapper, 'so I got all three.'

'Thanks for the knife, Snapper,' said Professor Leap,
flushed as punch.

DENIAL

Unable to regard the planning office with alarm or respect, Father had once designed a tower block which, during the official opening, shed a series of false walls to reveal a building which was quite pleasing to the eye. The embarrassed authorities finally faked a terrorist attack to remove the anomaly. Reluctant to give him any real remuneration, they loudly dismissed him as a genius. Father quit the scene, glutted with punishment.

He built the Hall on the site of an old country church, not in dedication but to prevent the church from happening again. The land was acquired with money he had printed himself when naively concerned about the national debt — in a brief and violent spasm of sagacity, Snapper had assured him it was none of his business. Father had been a tax-paying youth, yet to fully acknowledge his worth. 'I wish I had a fiver,' he would later laugh, 'for every time I earnt a fiver.'

He had long been curious at leaders' intermittent calls for a return to past values and had tested the notion by trying to build a house from the sky downwards. For the Hall he adopted a more successful form of reverse engineering. In a profound meditative state he saw a vision of Snapper pointing away and gasping 'You can't do *that!*' He was used to being told what he couldn't do after he had done it and recognised the vision as a glimpse of the future, boding success. If architecture was frozen music it was time it came out of the fridge. The Hall roofs were like open books, face-down and full of secrets. Rainwater was spluttered off by gargoyles who constantly yelled that they were scared of heights. A tower rose like a chimney for the release of surplus rage. The north wall was encrusted with three hundred individually-crafted barnacles, the rest disguised with ivy and granite. Father had weathered and aged each and every stone by smuggling it into a poetry recital.

Under the roofs were convolutive stairwells, vaulted chambers and walls deep enough to conceal more. There was a sharp turn for every ten yards and at each turn a novel effect. At one bend was a suit of armour containing a rotting grandad. Off a second a pedestal bore a vinyl globe, fat with emergency plasma. Around a third was an umbrella rack scabbarding a scrolled genealogy which proved that Hitler was a Jew. Central to the structure was the reading room, which topped a vortical drum like the whorl of a mechanical lead sharpener. One flight of stairs twisted upside-down and fed out of a window, to sort the men from the insects.

The Hall was carelessly furnished. Tangled mountains of chairs were draped in bladderwrack and bladed with plate fungus. In the sitting room was a piano — I once lifted the big lid and underneath was a whale-size ribcage and a lattice of muscles stretched like bubblegum. The keyboard lid was nailed permanently closed. The dining room was dominated by a large and luridly precise painting of a clown before a firing squad. As the years passed it was to echo the desolation of a burgeoning family at mealtime, as we stared at the erstwhile food set out for us. I remember one day that, as we were inspecting some soup which had the shape and resilience of a demolition ball, Father seemed worried. The omen of Snap's denial was the Hall's foundation-stone but the building was proving a beacon for mothfaced resenters and Snap had yet to say the magic words. Father feared the place was due to fall about his ears. We were oblivious to his concerns, having become deaf even to the gargoyles' mindboggling profanities.

What I alone didn't know as I grew up was that the Hall was a transcendence machine. Under tremendous pressure, Father finally held a demonstration for Snap who, his sparse hair wilding in the wind, pointed at the house. 'You can't do *that*!' he gasped. Father heaved a sigh of relief — he was onto a winner.

SHADOW

I had an imaginary playmate who bullied me constantly until I shoved him into the lake and held his head under. When the bubbles stopped I felt immensely relieved. The bastard had been making my life hell for years.

But I was appalled when Snapper reeled it out of the depths a week later. 'Nothing all day,' he said, packing up his gear in disgust. He slammed the tackle box on the kid's ear and conveyed the weightless, balloonlike body to the back porch, crashing it down. The body lay mauve and bloated amid the carp rods, its slitted eyes accusing. The last few days I'd been as happy as a spider in a firebucket and wasn't about to let this rotting phantom ruin my ease. When Snapper caught me opening the tackle box he barged me into Father's study. 'Raiding the gear!' he bellowed, causing a crack to jag across the ceiling.

'Wanted to catch some funny fish from the lake,' I said. 'Perhaps a relative. You've always said that when I was born Mother thought I was a coelacanth.'

'So she did,' said Father, nodding. 'It was a shock for us

all. Put the boy down, Snapper, and there's no call for the knife. The boy and I are going to the lake.'

By the light of a storm lamp I hooked the swollen kid onto the line with a mind to pitch it at the deeper waters. A strong wind was blowing. Father's line went into a tree, becoming tangled. As I tried to cast, the wind came up and gusted my imaginary playmate backwards into the night, breaking the line.

The next morning I discovered that the rotting kid was tagged on the roof like a stray piece of laundry. Rain was tumbling over it. I was out of Adrienne's window in a moment, crawling toward the black and splitting corpse. I had just tied its belt to mine when Snapper appeared at the window of his treehouse, transfigured with rage. 'It'll be a sad day for the devil when you see the light, laughing boy. Everything's in ruins because of your arrogance. So help me I'll come over there and smash your head like a snail!'

The granite jaws of a gargoyle closed on my ankle — I yanked myself free. 'You bastard,' it yelled. 'Lemme down. Lemme down or I'll be sick again.'

Clambering down the east wall toward poor Mr Cannon's window, I established a foothold which turned out to be the socket of poor Mr Cannon's eye. Letting out a scream, he held his face like an objet d'art until assured it was intact.

'An unprovoked attack,' yelled Snapper, having roared me into Father's study.

'What do you say is wrong with that?' I asked. 'He enjoyed it, and it didn't hurt me.'

'How can you stand for this boy's life?' demanded Snap. 'Clout him eighty-three times with a belt, brother.'

'Or a hose,' I suggested. But at this Snapper tore the belt from my waist, flipping the kid onto Father's desk. To my dismay the corpse's belly burst open, spewing maggots and slime onto architectural blueprints.

'Pulverise him with this,' shrieked Snap, brandishing the belt at Father, and began to laugh uncontrollably, his face scarlet.

'Are you alright, brother?' asked Father, frowning.

'Don't answer for my sake, Snap,' I said. 'I wouldn't slam an eyelid if you folded with a stroke.'

'Just fall the other way,' said Father, gesturing away from the desk.

'The desperate acts of this demon child are more important than your imploding *house!*' With a violent sweep of his arm Snapper sent everything flying from the desk — the body rocketed through an open window into a wheelbarrow trundled by Professor Leap.

'Leap!' I yelled through the window. 'There's an invisible corpse on the barrow!'

'Now listen to me, laughing boy,' he said, stopping and looking stormy. 'Just because you've turned your back on logic's province doesn't mean it isn't there.'

'And just because I say there's a rotting cadaver on the cart doesn't mean — Wait!' But he had given up and trundled on, shaking his head in dark disappointment.

'This is a fine joke you're playing on us all, eh boy?' chortled Father. 'A rotting child!'

'Madness is climbing the ladder of the boy's spine,' Snap was saying as I slipped from the room, 'and all you can do is sit there drumming like a clockwork chimp?'

The barrow stood empty at the back door. In the kitchen, Mother was carving up vegetables and the remains of the murdered boy. The body had been pulped as though beaten with a claw-hammer. 'Mother,' I stammered, shaking, 'what's for tea?'

She turned to me, a shred of gut dangling from her knife. 'Stew,' she said, and to this day I don't know whether she meant it as a noun or a verb.

My stomach revolved like a ferry, dumping its cargo with a splash.

'Laughing boy,' said Father's voice. My eyes opened upon my own room, its familiar chains and ring bolts. 'Collapsed in the kitchen — first sign of maturity. How you feeling?'

'As though I have been nailed to a rural door.'

'That's the spirit. Sit up, boy, and sip some of this. Hot broth.'

I had swallowed three spoonfuls when I saw the broken rib in the bowl.

But there was no sense in trying to speak to these people. So what if there was a rib? I took the bowl from Father and poured it away when he left. Thriving for two days on scraps of curtain, I soon felt ready for anything.

Calling on the Verger, I gave him a spud. 'Trying to bamboozle me again with votives?' he rumbled.

'And if I am?' I said. 'It's no secret I think you're useless. But seeing as you swan around in dark clobber and a hood I suppose you're the man.' I gave him a canvas bag containing all the remains I could salvage. 'Blather a bit of ceremonial pap over this and I'll stay out of your way for a year. Verger?'

He had gone. Squinting out of the window, I could see him already digging a hole half a mile away and nattering over a book.

The following winter I trudged to the burial site and lay some fishing weights on the grave. Brushing soft snow from the headstone, I read the simple epitaph:

> Here lies
> FREUD
> Rest in peace

SO WHAT

Adrienne found that deja vu could be induced by arranging to have a condescending moron tell her something she already knew. 'What's the use of that?' I asked, threading small predators into my hat and snapping the line.

She explained that the phantom events we recall during deja vu are enclosed in free-floating etheric bubbles squeezed off from the conscious time-stream whenever our time is wasted by vapid louts. She stated that some people had almost an entire lifetime stored up in deja vu timespace to compensate for an existence of abuse and distraction at the hands of the complacent. This much I already understood, and underwent a peculiar feeling of deja vu. But when Adrienne began to describe the fun of accessing and exploiting these auxiliary time nodes, the notion began seeping through the pale foliations of my brain. If several hundred deja vu experiences were lined up in a row and experienced as a seamless stream it would be akin to a clusterbursting hallucination. Whole months of wasted time would be given back to us in a single hit.

Me and Adrienne trooped off to Snapper's tree and called

up. 'Can we come in, Uncle Snap?'

A shutter opened and Snapper's vermilion face appeared. 'A man's home is his castle, you bastards!' he yelled. The statement was null and void because although true of Snapper's home it was untrue of those without defensive artillery.

'You're a bundle of nerves, Uncle.'

'So are we all when our muscle and bones are removed!'

Accurate and obvious, his remark roared us back to the moment at which it had first occurred to us. Adrienne had further to travel, being older, but we seemed to arrive almost instantly at a moment shortly before birth. The sensation lasted just a few seconds but it proved we were onto something.

Ofcourse we couldn't sit around provoking the drab from Snapper all day — we needed a means of drip-feeding retrogressive data at a steady and constant rate. I happened upon a Hemingway volume in the reading room and found it was perfect. At no point was there the risk of being jarred back into realtime by a new idea — the only problem was that once in deja vu timespace we would probably stop reading. So we asked Professor Leap to read the book into his tape recorder. Sitting in Adrienne's sanctuary room, we prepared ourselves and switched on the machine.

It was better than we expected. Some of the ideas went beyond the obvious into a kind of homicidal vacuum. I saw a riotous play of lights on my skullwall as the crucifying boredom ricocheted me out of the timestream. In what seemed like seconds I re-experienced the first few seconds of life and all of the author's ideas, then I was accelerating through a starfield of polymesmeric beauty. Skimming blurseas of red gold and deep flaring gardens, we were thrown across a sky, our shadows darting over the architecture of clouds which were soon streaking into smears. Huge tidal blurs were gashing wounds in space. Half my short life hit me like a thump in the chest as I passed through the sky, making it blink. For an instant, white space was speckled with black stars. I was learning and forgetting at a blur. I lost my body like a broken fingernail. The sparking pattern of passing stars resolved into a white revolving web and then into a sun which was everywhere. The universe opened like a flower, and we were gone. A billion miles below, the self-evident scrapped and sizzled like incinerating trash.

My eyes opened to the room and Adrienne's dazed, moon-pale face as the tape crackled and ended.

NANNY JACK

'Death,' my Father boomed, 'cancels everything but truth, then buries us in uncomfortable trousers and no underwear.' Nanny Jack kept death at bay by wielding her own scythe. She was a disquieting, chitin-hardened grandmother but she was all we had — I daresay on balance she was less spooky than a skeleton at a harpsichord.

But I'd be kidding if I were to deny the legacy of spine-igniting frights and traumas she bequeathed to the sensitive among us. Garping like a lizard, wilfully rattling, falling monumentally from casually-opened cupboards — these were the ways Nanny Jack made it known that she loved us. 'I wouldn't like to bump into *her* while stumbling drunk in a cat cemetery,' said Uncle Snapper on one occasion, unaware that Nanny Jack was standing behind him. That evening shrill screams echoed from the treehouse and in the morning a pasty Snapper denied unbidden that he had been 'dreaming of a thousand spiders'.

Nanny Jack said nothing at this or any other time — though on one occasion she gripped my arm, leant in close and made a sound like the hollow hiss in a conch shell.

When Mother told bedtime tales of a bogeyman which gathered boys to heaven by means of a hatchet I merely yawned. 'Well whatever it is,' I said, stretching, 'it can't be any more scary than Nan.' Mother tried to be angry but in truth Nanny Jack inspired in us all a kind of elemental terror. When she stood on the top stair, the shadow thrown on the landing wall was the spitting image of a praying mantis. When Professor Leap the lodger laid eyes on this, he locked himself away and finally emerged with a disturbing theory. 'Insects can camouflage themselves to look like leaves, branches and so forth,' he whispered urgently in the kitchen. 'Why not as an elderly relative?' And seeing Nanny Jack's beaked face at the window, he shrieked hoarsely and ran.

'Has anyone ever seen her walk from place to place?' muttered Snapper at another time, having called a conference behind the locked cellar door. He stood pop-eyed, breathing through his mouth. 'Doesn't she just seem to *be* in one place or another?'

Professor Leap leaned in under the bare lightbulb and expressed the view that she could flit about incredibly fast like a trapdoor spider. 'Does she ever eat?'

I spoke of the time I interrupted her eating coal out of the grate and how she had merely turned and snickered.

'She's dead,' said Professor Leap, 'petrified like a log. Including her behaviour.'

'You're talking about my mother-in-law,' said Father, nodding thoughtfully.

'Someone should ask her point-blank about it,' stated Adrienne, and we all felt a cloying fear.

'All she needs,' said Snapper quietly, 'is a priest to lock the grass over her head.'

Before we could harpoon him to a stop, Snapper was leaning on a spade in the light of an electrical storm and admiring a gravestone surmounted by a winged skull. 'If that doesn't provoke a reaction,' he said, 'I'll be a happy man.'

But Nanny Jack did react. By morning there was a clean hole in the gravetop and Snapper could not be coaxed from his tree — a trail of roots and earth had been trodden through the Hall.

Professor Leap was jubilant. 'Tracks!' He pointed like a vindicated explorer. 'Unbroken! From here' — the back door — 'to here.' The door of her room. Barely breathing, I put my ear to the oak panel and heard a rasping as of papery wings.

'Dead indeed,' said Father, uncertain and embarrassed.

'We have proved that she doesn't dart like a spider,' said Leap, aglow. 'And that's a start.'

I almost spoke of the sound I had heard through Nan's door but was prevented by the sudden entry of Uncle Snap with the keys to an industrial earthmover.

From then on we attempted to bury Nan pretty regularly — it was a family tradition. Needless to say we were unsuccessful and contracted a strange respect for our dormant elder. She would be gone the minute the hole was dug and be tracked down to the boisterous centre of a smoky saloon bar, or would begin to mime at the last moment, scaring us all. We could not conceal our admiration when a doctor who had called to sedate Snapper happened to seek a pulse in Nan's wrist and declared her dead, only to collapse of a seizure when she started to cackle. Our warmest moments of togetherness were those of Nan's return, when the entire household would gather nightshirted at the top of the stairs, watching the mantis shadow draw across the lower hall.

After one of these occasions, I listened again at her door and heard the scratchy flurring of paper. The following day, entering the room for the first time, I felt a paralysing anxiety. The furniture looked as if it could sting. What if I was discovered? Everything took on a demonic aspect. A giant book lay open on a table like a brooding moth. There was an inkwell and a quill. I frilled the pages — each bore the same, elegantly written words. 'Terror and dread, the claws of the soul — hang on for dear life.'

VIOLENT ACTING OUT

'Coming to the circus, laughing boy?'

'Not while I live.'

Why was I so surly as a child? On this occasion I was in the hot-house watering the brain tumours. The moment Snapper said 'circus' I was propelled like a crash dummy to an earlier year when I had run away to that establishment like the kid I was. Always of a serious disposition, I was also possessed of a resentment at having to grow while the world was losing its flavour. What little I'd surmised of it from a bedroom full of meathooks had led me to believe the last bastion of colour and integrity was sheltered by the big top. So before anyone noticed my absence I was sat in the audience watching a parade of cages circle the ring.

Bernard the Living Merchant. Old Scaly Gorgon. Terry the Human Constable. These are the sights I saw. I didn't know what other circuses were like but this one was teeming with psychotics. Gabbling men in make-up riding round and round on bicycles which were evidently too small for them. Chap in a leotard, biffing along a high-tension wire. Bloke dressed as the Joker, telling us everything was dangerous and real. As if I of all people didn't know. One fool struggled into a giant cannon — it was clear he had a deathwish and wasn't waiting for the gods to deliver. Nevertheless he gave a yell of surprise as he flew through the air. Meanwhile someone stepped into a cage with a lion. For me a lion is like any other situation — if you're going to whip it and push it away with a chair, why get involved in the first place? In my opinion the bloke was just doing it for show.

The true horrors, however, were the clowns. Ashen and demented, they shambled out of the wings like victims of an over-zealous bloodbank. Only the coldest of souls could watch their exploits without screaming. Car crashes, drownings, fires — you name it. Even the laughter was exaggerated. Some of them were carried off on stretchers which collapsed. The entire affair was meaningless, the stuff of nightmares. I had to get out.

So I was recovering outside when the tent sheet flapped like the blowing gown of an overworked surgeon and a strange, dilated clown lumbered out, hollering with laughter. It appeared that the fiend's trousers were filled with liquid. 'Hello, spuddling,' he roared. I remember I sank my teeth into his belly and a damburst of water flooded out, shrivelling the clown as he tried to staunch the flow. And to think I had considered joining these people.

Within minutes I was legging it through a maze of trailers and cages, pursued by a caterwauling bedlam of circus freaks. A clown on stilts told the rest where I was. I opened a trailer door, bursting in on a naked clown and a seal. Backing out, I overturned a trunk which vomited an avalanche of Masonic regalia. Panting steam, I set off through the animal boxes, flipping catches as I went and hearing screams behind me. If I hadn't the presence of mind to shove a juggler from a unicycle, would I be here today? Several clowns were injured by lions, a fact I have spent my life trying to regret. And arriving home, I found I had not been missed. I dismissed the episode as I would a slave.

Until Snapper entered the hot-house to tell me the circus was in town. I had no desire to get back on the horse and re-endure this particular trauma. If lightning doesn't strike twice we can dance in a storm in iron underwear. But Adrienne said it would be therapeutic and I allowed her to influence me. Off we all went to the circus.

Part of the reason was to get rid of our dog, Nelson, whose peculiarities were causing distress and would yield more money than war as a circus attraction. So while the others were elsewhere accosting the manager, me and my friend Billy Verlag were watching caged freaks circle the ring and I knew something was very wrong. Bernard the Living Merchant. Terry the Human Constable. And the clowns — here they were to remind us life was quaint and temporary. Thanks.

Billy was the only village kid who ever ventured onto the Hall grounds, being the only boy small and spherical enough for the other kids to boot over the perimeter wall. I think he looked up to me because I had told him about Hume's principle of unverified causality — that B follows A does not prove that A caused B. He had actually used this to get away with tripping up an old woman. Now he regarded the book I was holding. 'What's that?'

'Dostoevsky.'

'Can I have a go?'

I handed him the book, my eyes on the cavorting clowns.

They were looking horribly familiar — because they were the same ones as before. It was the same circus. And at that instant, they saw me. Miniature cars squealed to a halt. Painted faces stared out of a madman's universe.

The ringmaster's whip wrapped around my neck and, in an explosion of popcorn, I was dragged like a cur into the ring. Elephants were circling and I had to roll to avoid being trampled as the ringmaster ordered the clowns to 'terminate' me. That was the word he used. I pushed a clown out of its miniature car and led the others a merry dance until I crashed into a barrel and they pounced, two clowns holding me by the arms while a third beat the bejesus out of me. The audience loved this. Maybe they thought I was a midget. The applause was deafening as I was loaded into the cannon, which stank of gunpowder. I don't remember anything between then and the moment I awoke in an adjoining field. Everything was totally unreal — I felt like a statistic.

When the others got home with Nelson in tow they asked me where I'd disappeared to. It turns out Billy Verlag had been so absorbed in *The Idiot* he hadn't noticed my ordeal — thought I'd gone for a slash or something. Even Adrienne was sceptical. What about the bruises?

A wound heals slower than a kiss. When I'm advised to cheer up because it may never happen I'm reminded that it has and may again. The most amusing thing about a pantomime horse is the necessity of having to shoot it twice.

That's my story and I'm sticking to it.

ISLAND

I told Billy Verlag I intended to explore the island at the centre of the lake and that I'd need him for ballast. Of all the territory bought with my Father's forged money the lake was the strangest. It was rumoured to contain jet-propelled herring and trout which could imitate your facial expressions. But the island was a mystery.

'Don't ask me to take you there,' said Father. 'You'll only start looking at the sky in a funny way and beg to go for a drive.'

Mutinous with curiosity, I peered through the telescope in Adrienne's attic but could make out only a few shrubs. 'You don't want to go there,' said Adrienne, lazily swinging one long leg from her sleeping-hammock. 'Especially with little Verlag. I went, and may never understand what I saw.'

That was enough for me. One afternoon when everyone was off burying Nan, Billy hurtled over the perimeter wall and we went immediately to the lake, pushing out on a wooden palette. 'Charon the ferryman did this,' I said, pushing at the raft-pole. 'Demanded hard cash though he was clearly nothing more than a skeleton. Must have been *some* tissue clung in that skull of his.'

There was a scraping sound under the raft, which Billy instantly attributed to a sawfish dragging its nose across the hull. 'Nonsense,' I said, and peered into the water. The lake was infested with boss-eyed cartoon characters which ghosted up, stared like lost souls and dipped away again. Inbetween were swirling volume levels and swarms of seahorses with tiny training wheels.

'What is it then?' asked Billy fearfully.

'You're right,' I said, punting again. 'It is a sawfish.'

Our dodgy vessel was tipping alarmingly and we were only halfway across. 'Slow down,' sobbed Billy.

'Don't worry,' I said. 'There's no prejudice against fat little blighters out here. I reckon these strange fish will take to you like pigs to garbage.'

Billy released acoustically garish screams and I was soon vaulting through hoops to comfort him.

'Think of the pirates,' I said, kicking an errant moray into the depths. 'They used to drag out eachother's innards and set them alight.'

Billy calmed down, wiping his eyes. 'Why?' he croaked, sniffing.

I shrugged. 'To make everyone's existence a living hell.'

Billy bawled in horror and misery as we pitched through a frothing maelstrom of disquieting critters. The water was now too deep for the staff and we had to paddle our hands in the water. I had begun to wish I had gone with the others to sling some turf over Nanny Jack — then the water shallowed out and Billy's screams began to echo off the bank of the island. Reaching shore, we dragged the raft onto the mud and gazed around.

The island was about sixty foot square and covered in the dullest bushes I had ever seen. 'So what?' said Billy, breaking a branch and tossing it away impatiently.

I tripped over and swore in a temple language known only to Adrienne and myself — I had scattered pieces of a kid's fort built from lollipop sticks. Looking closer I realised it was a tiny wooden fence, extending parallel with the shore. 'Is this yours, Verlag?' I demanded, pointing. Billy looked at the little broken wall, waiting for a thought as for the second coming. We followed the structure a way — it seemed to encircle the island — and Billy started gibbering with an unaccountable fear. I tried to calm him by talking about the great explorers but he saw only the danger in the enterprise. 'Verlag,' I said, 'yours is a narrow range of experience and in the age of exploration that's the spice. The American Indians discovered America every time they glanced up. The Chinese found the environment too abrasive for homes of gum and wafer, which as you know were the farcical materials they favoured at the time. The Icelanders liked the place so much they never told anyone about it. But somehow everyone stumbled into it at one time or another. When Columbus finally got there he was mistaken for a god because he was the only person on Earth the natives hadn't met. No wonder he became obsessed with spuds and —'

'Sh-sh-shut *up*, laughing boy,' stammered Billy plaintively, and pointed at the undergrowth.

In the centre of the island, hidden amid greenery, was a miniature house.

It was the Hall, surrounded by bonsai trees, next to an inland pool representing the lake. Billy and me spent ages exploring this tiny landscape, which seemed perfect in every detail — the little structure I had kicked through was the perimeter wall.

The pool even had an imitation island in the middle. Splashing over and crouching down, I was not a little amazed to see that this small island, too, bore a model reproduction of the Hall and grounds. This Hall was the size of a matchbox, next to a lake the size of a plate. At this lake's centre was an even smaller island.

I stood, looking around, and underwent a sensation of telescoping vertigo — the Hall stood in the distance, tiny as a matchbox. I was trembling like a leaf. Billy was at my side, frowning down at the island with unusual concentration — his expression grew strained as the idea ripened. We looked up at the sky as one, to see if giant boys were frowning down at us.

I asked for the magnifying glass which Billy used to start fires, and focused on the plate-sized lake, the thumb-sized island. I heard Billy snuffling as the fish-eye blur zoomed into focus on a satellite-picture of a mini-house, a droplet-lake and a dot-island. We stood up from this diabolical micro-circuit. I had arrived ready for anything but the inconceivable. At what scale were we? Was the Hall a model ending at the perimeter fence? Where was the real me? 'What *level* is this?' I demanded, my voice cracking, and we began the sort of synchronised scream which children can do with such ease. My skull shrieked through my skin, like the Munch painting of that idiot screaming on Hastings pier.

Bats out of hell, we paddled away from the island, casting fearful looks at the sky.

When Father found us huddling in a ditch under a tarpaulin sheet he was instantly apprised. 'Oho,' he said. 'So you went to the island.'

'Take us to the village, Father,' I begged. 'Is there anything outside the fence?'

He laughed amiably and said he'd just been in the village.

'How did you know we went to the island?' asked Billy, blowing his nose.

'It's obvious,' he said, and I thought he was referring to our shuddering fright. But he said he knew it as soon as he got back and saw a huge hole in the perimeter wall and a log which appeared to have been snapped in half and tossed aside by a giant.

SKELETON CREW

Uncle Burst was no uncle but a tin-eared buffoon who quietly considered our table and food a sacrament to his grandeur. His presence was permanent and no one recalled how it had begun. God alone knows what slobbering fiends inhabited the unexplored planet of his head — long silences obscured this aspect of his personality. But on occasion he would look up, his face displaying a wily and distorted power. With the best will in the world we could not ignore Burst's remarks at these times. His notions were as inconspicuous as underpants on a bayonet.

'This chops of mine,' he said one day as we were sat in the garden. He rubbed his chin as though considering a shave. 'Jowls, forehead, eyes — the whole dismal jamboree. Made of pasta, all of it.'

We sat absolutely still. Even Snapper, who was wont to go bonkers at the sigh of an ant, froze in the act of polishing his gun.

There was a pause during which the summer hum approached a deafening pitch.

'Isn't it a free world?' Burst shouted suddenly, as if we

had spoken. 'Aren't I entitled like everyone else?'

'It's not quite a matter of entitlement,' said Father carefully. 'Pasta, you say?'

'Flour and water, yes,' said Burst curtly.

Struggling, Father attempted a judicial expression. 'I'm sure there must be a precedent for this business, Burst,' he said. 'What does history teach us —'

'That I'm the cat's pyjamas,' stated Burst, and stared at him with a wall-eyed, brutal face.

'He's due for the laughing academy, *that*'s what we all know!' yelled Uncle Snapper, and ran as Burst stood.

Burst tackled him by the legs, spilling him onto the lawn and yapping like a dog in a cyclone cellar. 'Shoot him!' Snapper shrieked, pointing at the rifle.

'No good, Snapper,' said Father mildly, pouring another scotch. 'Can't kill a man who isn't flesh and blood.'

That evening Snapper sneaked into Burst's bedroom with a fork. 'We'll soon see who's made of pasta and who isn't,' he said, and woke Burst with his laughter.

The next morning Snapper was lying tense and motionless in a hammock which I now know to have been an enormous sling, and passing the study I heard Father's wise voice through the thick oak door. 'There are certain places, Burst, where pasta is neither needed nor desired, such as in an otherwise authentic salad. Take my good advice sir, and put aside this facial obsession — you are scaring my son and daughter.'

I did not linger to hear Burst's response, but he remained bashful and withdrawn for several weeks.

It was my misfortune to be alone with Burst when he perked up at the dinner table and announced he was beyond analysis. The others were in the hills trying to bury Nan and, seeming to have no choice in the matter, I listened in silence. He stated the opinion that there was a front part of him and a back part, and that this rendered him intangible to the common man. 'No observation of me from any one angle,' he muttered gruffly, spooning gravy into his gob, 'can provide a complete picture. Only over time, after viewing me from many bearings, can a full mental image be generated.'

He sopped the gravy dregs with a crust. 'And even that idea of my appearance,' he continued, 'leaves so much to be desired.'

To illustrate the point he instructed me to make four sketches of him standing by the lake. On rifling through the results and finding that front, back, left and right were correct in every detail, he bellowed with annoyance and tore them to pieces.

'Boy,' he said later, still flustered, 'do not tell your father or anyone about that experiment. Nobody would care or understand.'

Weeks after the household's despondent return from the hills with Nan, we were striving to eat the evening meal. All was silent save for the clink of cutlery and an occasional, frantic prayer — until Burst nailed his colours to the mast.

'My skeleton,' he announced, with meaning, 'is all it should be.' Then he looked sharply at all present as though daring us to challenge him.

It became clear that Burst considered his skeleton the eighth wonder. He spoke of it until we could barely see, boasting that it was fantastic. With the arrogance of a monarch he claimed that it formed the Japanese pictogram for 'public telephone' when exposed to X-rays.

This cavalier attitude to endostructure was the last straw

as far as Father was concerned and he hissed chapter and verse to Burst as we crept into the hospital. It has occurred to me since that the X-ray machine in the storeroom may not have been in working order but at the time we were bewildered to find that Burst's chest contained nothing in the way of dense tissue or anything else — the image was as blank as a winter sky.

'Stand aside,' shouted Father, shoving Burst away and standing at the exposure plate. To his complete dismay the result showed a priceless Penny Black at the juncture of his sternum. Startled, the Verger punched him aside. His own chest seemed to bear the landplan of a flyover which would obliterate the natural and historic beauty of the local area. Professor Leap could detect an ongoing Napoleonic sea confrontation in his image, and disturbingly visible in Nanny Jack's was the shadow of a giant praying mantis. Adrienne's entire torso housed a daguerreotype of Ezra Pound being forcibly restrained by psychiatric nurses. Examining my own X-ray I could discern only a church steeple, a Hinton hypercube and a convulsing Apache. We had to wrestle Uncle Snapper against the plate and the combined effect of the entire group struggling within the frame produced a kaleidoscopic montage of the 50,000 American GIs who went AWOL in Second World War Europe.

Leaning in a corner with smugly folded arms, Burst asked us rhetorically whether these were the musculo-skeletal systems appropriate to civilised men.

Gathering our wits with litter-spikes, we went home and resolved never to think about our skeletons again — naively forgetting that our skeletons would make their presence felt whether we liked it or not.

STAGE

I'm all for education but not when it entails being glared at by a pair of eyes behind which there is no brain. There are few lessons to be learned under a moron's tutelage and foremost among them are degradation and fantasies of homicide — skills I consider unworthy even of a chef.

Mother once suggested that a school curriculum would slow my learning to a manageable rate and the next morning Father took me reluctantly to school. Whenever one of us entered the village, women swept children from the street, bicycles were abandoned, windows were slammed shut and ineffectual shopkeepers stood armed and apprehensive in doorways. But today this was raised to the tenth power — I felt like the previously unseen mutant child of a newly-defiant workman. One villager lobbed a lump of garlic, which I caught in my mouth. On arriving at the school I was asked to chalk my name on the blackboard for all to see and I struck up BEELZEBUB in elaborate gothic script, making some of the more timid children scream. Later I was hauled up for writing when I was meant to be guzzling milk and was told to read my scribbles to the rest of the class:

> TED HUGHES' SCHOOLDAYS
> A crocodile died for my satchel —
> tearful ears of sedative
> pierced a carapace
> to leave a leering dead weight
> and a hateful, glossy case

The mauve-faced teacher snatched it away before I could continue. Only Billy Verlag was snorting with laughter. My first and last day at primary school smashed to an end when I begged the headmistress to beat me as hard as I knew she wanted to. It was decided that I should be educated at home by Professor Leap.

Leap was a fiercely complex personality. If his innards were removed, unravelled and stretched taut, I'd be the last to assign blame. A man of incoherent views and boundless energy, he had fled the medley of assassination attempts which are among the distressing hazards of academic life. Presented with myself snaffling in a cage, Leap launched a three-pronged assault, each prong as dreary as the next. By the light of a single candle he would moon around in a cloak and sing mournful dirges while strumming a lute:

> I mime amid the crows and fog,
> Concluding with a groan —
> The only watcher was a dog
> Whose snout was dripping foam.

During these dismal interludes I was a sleeping volcano, waiting to blast forth a flood of indifference. 'What images does the music bring to mind?' he asked, and I described a vision I had experienced of Leap creaking from a rope and undergoing his final, boring spasm.

The second prong was history and propaganda. 'What was it,' he asked, 'that enabled the English to travel the world, taking control of every land they encountered?'

'Bad manners.'

'I was thinking not of a guiding principle but a skill. For what was England celebrated?'

'Farce?'

I meant that it was a nation made from farce's ingredients but at that age I could not express myself with such clarity. Leap made allowances and switched to the third prong of his programme — philosophy. 'If everyone else in the world leapt off a cliff, what would *you* do?'

'Celebrate.'

'Progress is a bit thorny,' I heard Leap telling Father under my window one evening. 'I don't suppose we can drown the bugger?'

'Your guess is as good as mine.'

And so it went on, sustained by my assertion that Spinoza made his living as a professional clown and Leap's frustration at being unable to find any evidence to the contrary. Then one day Leap had a blinder of an idea — we would attend the opera. I was all for it, and Leap was soon driving Adrienne and me through the countryside and insisting that he could spy 'something beginning with *T* '.

'Trudging mourners?'

'No.'

'Telepathically spooky youngsters?'

'No.'

'Twitching centipedes?'

'I *beg* your pardon?'

'What, then?'

'Trees. *Trees*, that's all!'

At the theatre we witnessed a display which I daresay civilised cultures disallow by law. Otter-eyed, snivelling opera singers wailed nonsensical laments which, upon subsequent translation, I discovered to be a tissue of lies. One had been moaning about a dragon. The entire affair had been a waste of time.

But on the night I was not to know this — all I could do was stare in disbelief as a squad of bloated louts tried to make enough noise to convince us something was happening. Within minutes I was prepared to gnaw off a leg to escape. The audience seemed to be in a state of keen amazement or bitter concentration. On one side of me Professor Leap sat still as a pillar of salt. I turned to Adrienne — she looked at me sideways like a turbot, and I knew we were undergoing similar torture.

On stage it seemed that for half an hour a man with a beard had been deciding what to order in a restaurant, and was yelling every twang of prevarication at the top of his lungs. I was twitching like a convict in the hotseat — all my restraint turned to fog. 'The steak, you bastard,' I yelled, 'have the steak and get on with it!' Professor Leap parped like a punctured gas-line, trembling with pressurised rage as all eyes turned our way. I suppose the bearded man was used to this sort of outburst as he barely reacted, and perhaps welcomed any distraction from his embarrassing exhibition. He was now sat at the table sobbing at his weakness and lack of will. I rolled something from the corner of my eye which resembled a fragment of toast. 'What about this?' I bellowed, standing, and hurled it so that it bounced across the table. 'Eat this if you can! It's better than you deserve for boring the shit out of every bastard here!' In a genuine attempt to contain laughter, Adrienne pursed her lips tight and let out what sounded like a florid raspberry. The bearded man was stood looking up at us in anger, fists balled on hips. The audience, which had previously glared as though holding my doom in reserve, now regarded me with a farmer's loathing and began to rise. 'Go ahead, you spoon-fed idiots!' I roared. 'Cluttering the world with your inanities!'

'The boy doesn't mean it,' squeaked Leap, standing in fright to assure them. 'He's just very, very bored.'

It was a full four months before our bandages were removed, and for a full year Professor Leap shrieked when he saw me, which was many times a day. He began going around belligerently untrousered and was discovered one night crouching naked on the porch roof, torn by rain.

God help those who sit through the *whole* of the Ring. When I desire a spectacle I look to my own conscience. Glancing back I see that my reaction to opera was reserved, considering what it has cost me in trauma and grief. We have truth in order not to die of art.

LIAR

My mother was an insane and matronly lady with two sky-blue eyes which she claimed were interchangeable. And she sat at my bedside formulating tales which I now understand were meant to fire my imagination and slam me into nightmares so inescapable as to make *The Trial* look like *The Clangers*. She had my undivided attention as she described a spectral, nocturnal intruder, garlanded with entrails, beaked, fishfaced and wearing a turban. When I asked in undisguised wonderment why it wore a turban she said 'To hide its glowing brain.' Apparently this impetuous ghoul biffed its way into kids' bedrooms and took the occupants free of charge to some farcical underworld, where even the most compliant brat was submitted to baleful tortures. Mother stated with absolute conviction that the brute was brimming over with lubrication and unnecessary thoracic legs. She said hide under the covers when you hear the frilling of its gills, watch out for its utensil hands, don't even try to locate its arse, and so on.

Well it was clear we couldn't have a thing like that running around and I resolved to trap and kill the beast using every ruse at my command. One of the things Mother always emphasised was that the creature only sprang into view when a child had been misbehaving. In order to lure the beast I would have to provoke some kind of ruck and I decided to belt Uncle Snapper in the eye to kick off the campaign. Clutching at his face and bellowing for assistance, Snapper flushed like a blood orange. Everyone piled in to spectate his flailing distress. 'This flaunting idiot claims the right to ignore every moral code which inconveniences him!' he yelled. 'He's just this second belted me in the face!'

At this Father swelled with pride and pleasure. 'Good boy,' he said.

'But Dad, look!' I cried, kicking Snapper expansively in the balls. The onlookers began to laugh and applaud, already composing the tale for the mirth of future generations.

Father was chuffed and encouraging. 'No need for concern, Snapper. He'll tire of it eventually.'

At three in the afternoon I told the Verger exactly what I thought of him and his way of life. The Verger smiled and took me aside — in fact I was taken so far aside I ended up in the lake. 'It's better than you deserve, boy!' he hollered from the shoreline.

'I don't love it or even like it!' I yelled, sputtering as I trod water. 'Snap said you were a crippling burden on our leisure and joy — he wrote down every seditious word. Said I should memorise it — say it to you without pulling any punches.'

The Verger was operatically apprised, adopting the stance of a fierce Victorian balloonist. 'Oho! So Colonel Blimp's funnelling his malice!'

'Yes sir,' I said, swallowing and coughing water. 'Had everyone convinced you should go and take your creaking sagacity with you. Whole household was behind him, urging him on with word and gesture. I drew the short straw. Tried to hide but they dragged me out by the legs. Don't be angry, sir — they're uneducated and mired in hopeless lust.'

The Verger strode off with a set expression, rolling up his sleeves and fists.

He happened to encounter Father first. Father was reading the paper when the Verger entered, austere and glowering. 'So the whole household thinks I'm an acute picture of parsimonious reserve and as abruptly shootable as a town crier, is that it?'

Father looked up, mildly. 'Well now that you mention it, yes.'

'On my ruddy bum I am!' shouted the Verger with a compressed bellicosity.

As I slapped ashore a blue light pulsed across the landscape — the Verger speeding to hospital in an armoured van.

'Snapper,' said Father during the evening meal. 'Imagine my disappointment this afternoon when the Verger went bonkers.'

'Eh?' said Snapper, perplexed.

'I had hoped that your fooling days were over. Then the Verger, poor man, flies off his hinges.' He looked at Snapper coldly. 'Am I understood?'

It was getting dark and I was not yet disgraced.

'Congratulations, Mother,' I said, 'you have constructed this meal with a cunning and ruthless evil.'

Everyone agreed. 'The bacon's like chainmail,' remarked

Professor Leap.

'And this fish is as fresh as a newborn,' said Adrienne.

'The gills are still working on mine. At least she covered it with cress so as not to distress us. It seems about to cry.'

'Look at the bloody bite-radius on the thing,' urged poor Mr Cannon. 'And what's this? Cartilage? What are you making of that, Professor?'

'I do believe Cannon that you have discovered the unhappy sod's swim bladder.'

After dinner I was taken aside by Father. 'Trying to keep order in this cracked house is like trying to bury your grandmother,' he said. 'Difficult and distressing, yet one of the activities I crave though it exhausts me. You, lad, are the civilising force I never dared hope for. Non-pious honesty. This is the proudest day of my life.'

The long and the short of it is this — despite my having kicked Snapper in the balls, implicated Snapper in the Verger's breakdown, set fire to the curtains and blamed Snapper, shot at Snapper, boxed the ears of Snapper, roared abuse at Snapper, reversed over Snapper and cackled at Snapper, it seemed that as far as everyone was concerned I had spent the day behaving myself until I was raw.

That night I lay in bed as Mother read a story about a dog who went to the moon. 'And good riddance,' she concluded, shutting the book.

'But before I settle down,' I said, 'I've got something to show you.' And cupping both hands to my nose, I blew out a snotpile resembling pulverised kale.

Mother shrieked like a parson.

'It's perfectly legit, mother.'

'You *evil* child!' she screamed. 'You'll lock antlers with the monster I've mentioned for the *terrors* you enjoy!'

After Mother had pushed off I lay in wait for the phantom, which I had privately concluded was some kind of mutant, like Dumbo. My vigil was rewarded. At midnight a sinister shadow entered the room, its head clinking the mobile I had made from dried anchovies. Loitering and ragged, it stepped into the snare and was flung upside down, dropping several knives and making sounds which were frankly tedious and uninspired. The whole household burst in with guns at the ready as I hit the light and took aim with a Beretta and a Smith .38. Ofcourse the honking and flipping aberration suspended before us was Uncle Snapper, bent on revenge. More surprisingly, Mother was carrying a cake with eight candles as the household gathered at my bed-end singing 'Happy Birthday'. Father pinned a target to Snapper's back.

MISTER HIERONYMUS

In fact there was a real bogeyman which my family had been seeing for generations and which they called Mister Hieronymus. Supposedly it appeared at moments of dangerous portent, such as my own birth — everyone asserted Hieronymus had delivered me. Its blurred image appears in a murky sepia-tint of my great grandfather, who is sat blithe on a bicycle — behind him a gaunt figure stands like a human pterodactyl.

But the first encounter I recall was caused by Professor Leap. He was culturing a sample of his nerves and the result was a tangle of microthin wires like an industrial art exhibit. It almost became potbound and Leap removed it to the hot-house, where he had set up a nutrient vat. 'No sense experimenting with nerves or anything else when they're in *my* body,' he explained, flushed with laughter. 'But these beauties? Look at 'em!'

This was all fine and dandy until he decided to run a nerve bundle from the hot-house, across the yard and into his arm. 'This way,' he said, bedding down in the dining room, 'I can feel things when I'm not even there.' We told him he wouldn't feel anything but the tickle of greenfly but he didn't care — he liked the idea of having a conscious process occurring outside his body.

The experiment was carried out at night to reduce the likelihood of someone kicking through the nerve lead. But it seemed the family phantom was never far from the Hall — it blundered into the hot-house and became entangled, making itself known like a chicken snagged on a barbed-wire fence. Professor Leap was shot through with horror vibes, his hair turning instantly white. Mister Hieronymus was wired into his system, filling him with visions of spinelight, sub-terranean scabgardens and yellow voltaic pain. Leap saw children lost spectacularly in nursery forges. Hieronymus thrashed in the nerve net, firing images of blown ghost and the unravelling dead. Leap yanked the suture-plug from his arm and lay trembling, veins hammering like fists.

In the morning the snow-haired Leap couldn't stop shaking. He pointed at a window and said he saw tatters of devil flapping there. Snapper was unsympathetic and appalled. 'This nerve farm of yours has served as a betsy lamp — we'll have moaning glowheads converging on us from miles around. *God* almighty!'

'Mind you,' began Father.

'Don't *encourage* him!' yelled Snapper, astonished and exasperated.

The dense mesh in the hot-house had been warped by the intrusion. 'What if it's still in there?' whispered Leap, trembling. 'I daren't plug in again.'

'This ganglia should be destroyed by fire,' bellowed Snapper. 'Verger, back me up on this — *nerves?*'

The Verger pulled up the hood of his robe, his face extinguishing in shadow.

'Well I for one think it's the spice,' I said, barely registering Adrienne's slow, stern, meaningful shake of the head. 'And I'll plug into this mess like the fierce one I am.'

'There's no guarantee my nerves won't cause a rejection,' said Leap eagerly.

'Won't be the first time, Leap,' said Father amiably and we all laughed.

All except Snapper, who couldn't believe what I can only describe as his ears. 'You can joke about this eh? You can stand and roar. Well by god you'll know the full extent when the Artless Dodger here has a meeting of minds. He may have been delivered by the bastard but a special relationship? With that thing?'

I really didn't know what I was doing — mainlining a spectre isn't wise. But I'd been having end-of-the-world dreams since I was three — if anyone could take it, I could. Hooked into the nerve cable I lay awake in a sleeping bag. 'Break a leg, laughing boy,' said Father, going off to bed. 'And take a gander at the marrow if you get a chance — looks like pepperoni.'

Hours passed like night clouds. I had become forgetful and sleepy. Then the atmosphere shifted. There was a gust of wind — a door slammed like a menu being returned to a waiter. I was approaching the jump ledge of Hieronymus's sidelong world. The room exploded in my face. I suppose being young I was more tolerant of having my brain torn like a paper bag and after a few preliminary horrors I was sat on the shore of an electrocutive river, my body anchored to the land by a muscle web reminiscent of melted pizza string. Mister Hieronymus was beside me and believe me it was weird. Brows like shoulderblades. Sternum and ribspread like a crab's underside. Soul flooded with poison.

'That beak of yours,' I said and, realising I had been whispering, bellowed as though at a foreigner. 'That beak of yours. Iconoclastic. Max Ernst. *Mythological Woman*. I like it.'

'Many have,' it said, 'and lived.'

'Broken skin,' I said. 'Nice one.'

'Laughing boy, we go back a long way — I delivered you. And I was worried when the Professor felt willing to use you for his experiment — he has a forehead like a dirigible and for a few bob he'd flog his aunt and shadow. But I know how stubborn you are so we may as well get this over with.'

'What's the deal?'

'Things occurring behind the freakshow scenes of the Hall. Things in which you are not included.'

'You mean Nan's funerals? I'm going to the next one though I don't care to — I've told them in every bloody language but improvisational mime.'

'I know — but it's not that. I daresay it'll cause a rift but I'll be judged by god and my peers — none of whose existence I have been able to verify. Fact is, laughing boy, the Hall is building a quantum of energy to be released subsequently in an audacious crescendo. Pulling out the stops as it were. Getting uncomfortable?'

Every atom of the landscape hurt — each man has his share of pain but searing agony smacks of decadence. 'I want to hear it.'

'So we have a transcendence operation,' it continued. I realised that it was fishing — a thread trailed from the high-voltage river into Hieronymus's mouth and it was hauling in the line by swallowing periodically. Whatever it had caught was nearing the surface. 'Live and let live, laughing boy. Keep your head down if you have to dig a hole to do so. You sense your own importance far beyond the human range. Life's a carousel with skeleton horses. And you're aware the motivating force behind the universe is —'

A burst of static and I was back in the dining room — Snapper stood before me with a flaming torch in one hand and the pulled plug in the other. Behind him was a fiery glow. 'If god wanted us to cultivate our nerves,' he roared, 'he would have told us not to.'

I pushed past him and he followed across the yard. The hot-house was a halloweenhead. Windows popped and the roof exploded, flames belching through. Inside, nerves curled and burnt like nettles.

THUMPING DOUGH

Occasions of trial and forbearance for one and all were the visits from Father's vexingly exuberant cousin, Roger Lang. Sometimes when speaking of him, Father would become uncharacteristically pop-eyed and begin strangling empty air. I remember one occasion when Roger turned up yelling like Santa and expecting us to respond. Me and Adrienne crept halfway down the stairs and saw him shouting toward Father in the hallway. 'Good heavens old man, this place of yours is a gothic nightmare. A few ornamental fiends and Bob's your uncle. Speaking of which.' And he tore the wrapping from a huge mounted moose-head at which Father stared in appalled astonishment.

'A cow.'

'I prefer to think of it as a moose, old fellow — and the best of its type I've ever come across. Quite a find really. It's been sat on a barrel in an unsuccessful fruiterers for the last six years and the shopkeeper was arrested the other week for going mad — said the blessed thing kept shouting at him and trying to run things. In fine condition though.

Name's Ramone. Eyes are quartz crystal, and those antlers are tough enough to swing on. I believe it even salivates.'

Father was doubtful. 'Yes, well the benefits of having a dribbling wildebeest forever mournfully regarding one are dubious at the best of times.'

Lang looked at Father as though at a madman. 'Dubious? Why the benefits my dear fellow are legion. I'll hang it on the hook here, shall I?'

'If you have strong feelings on the matter.'

Lang placed the bleak-featured head on the hallway wall. 'Now — where are those brats of yours? There they are — Alice and the Little Prince!'

'That animal head is rotting from the inside,' I stated, walking solemnly down.

'Like Roger's principles,' stated Adrienne, following after.

'Antlers like radar,' I muttered.

'Perhaps it'll whisper the racing results,' muttered Adrienne.

'Crack your face, you two,' chortled Roger like a toytown mayor. 'You've got to laugh otherwise you'll cry.'

'I see no impediment to doing both at once,' said Adrienne, looking expressionlessly up at the moose-head. Then she turned, giving Roger a scornful glance, and walked back upstairs.

'Did it relinquish its bonce by choice?' I asked, regarding the head.

'Ha, ha — nice one, Scooter,' he laughed, fuzzing my hair.

'Don't *ever*,' I emphasised murderously, 'call me Scooter again.' And I marched away.

Roger took a spare room and toured the house like a

stranger. His routine rejection of the facts allowed him to be surprised by the same ones repeatedly. 'Listen old man,' he said to Father, pouring port, 'I've just been in the west wing — entered a room back there and interrupted a nun in a welding mask. What's the story?'

'You know very well what the story is, Roger,' said Father tiredly. 'They bother no one.'

'D'you mean to say you countenance these extraordinary practices?'

Father sighed, his eyes filming over.

The moose was beginning to salivate, forming a pool on the carpet like the slime of a snail. Snapper took Father aside and whispered urgently. 'We can't tolerate a gobbing mammal like this all day every day. It'll start pursing its lips — expressing itself. It'll come alive and terrorise the creatures which belong here.'

'It's a gift, brother.'

'Roger's a hound in all but name,' said Snapper. He kicked at the slime. 'Look at this. He'd harness a wren to pull a houseboat. Get rid of him, brother.'

'Secret assignations?' smiled Lang, appearing in the hallway, and Snapper made a brisk exit. Lang idled at the moose-head, admiring it as Father stood awkwardly by. 'A curious point which you will scarcely believe is that this artefact requires occasional feeding.'

'How,' asked Father, 'occasional?'

'Only once an hour, old soak,' beamed Roger. 'With grain. Let's take a turn round the grounds and I'll state my plan.'

'The whole front area,' Lang announced as he and Father strolled in the twilight, 'will be given over to containers of trash. The house itself will be coated in an industrial laminate and will glint like a moonbathing slug. Below is the wood, full of frenzied wildlife — this area I shall burn to ashes, and pave over with a giant likeness of my own chin, viewable from this hill. Everything from the far shore to the perimeter will be used for sport.'

'Sport?' mumbled Father as if in a dream, seeing only moonlight and the fine trace of shadow trees.

'Windsurfing old boy, sailing — anything where acrobatic youngsters wear bright clobber. This soil-infested mire just isn't you.'

Normally the soul of patience, Father found his benevolent stability giving way to a contained rage.

In the hallway the next morning, Snapper was stuffing handfuls of grain into the moose's mouth and sobbing with the stress of its demands.

'Glad you told me to get into the architects' lark, old man,' said Roger gustily in the drawing room, helping himself to the contents of the drinks cabinet. Father had once remarked offhand that the day complacent, blinkered louts like Roger Lang got into the architects' game the human spirit would fade like an ember. Roger had taken this as an archaically-phrased nugget of advice. 'Only last week I finished punching a hole in that gaff on the coast you designed — turned it into a hypermart and a bowling alley.'

'The cottage?'

'Took some doing,' said Roger, swallowing port and gesturing at the wall. 'You'll want to knock this through. When do you want it done?'

'When hell freezes over.'

'I sense resistance.'

'So did the Nazis.'

'Ha, ha — calm down old boy — give us a smile.'

'Drop dead and I'll laugh.'

'Ha, ha, ha — you slay me.'

'I will.'

'Ha, ha, ha.'

'And here's the knife I'll do it with you bastard.'

'Ha, ha, ha.'

But Roger's blithe, intimidating jollity confounded our efforts at homicide. He even made vapid remarks in his sleep. One night Snapper sneaked in and pressed a pillow over Lang's face, breaking his nose. Another time Mother caught him offguard and whapped him round the face with a trout. I myself interrupted a dismal coin trick by belting him in the belly with a crowbar. And all he could ever do was forgive us.

Father was knelt on the floor shaving his shadow when he heard a rumpus and went into the hallway. Uncle Burst had skidded in the phlegm, hit the ceiling and woken up — Snapper was having to keep him at bay with wild swings of a cargo hook. 'I've every right to walk with your legs,' Burst was shouting, and Snapper's strained, tear-rashed face was a silent plea for release.

Father found he didn't have to enter the drawing room to address his cousin — there was a hole in the wall through which Roger could be seen leaning cheerfully on a sledgehammer. 'Spawn of *hell*!' gasped Father.

'So am I, if it's any consolation.'

Father stepped swiftly back and forth through the gap. 'Why, Roger, why?'

'A bit of a joke, that's all.'

'The bit that isn't funny,' Father emphasised, and Roger laughed good-naturedly. Father's eyes were red as stop signs. 'Not only have you hung up a moose's face for the purpose of being crammed with grain but you've enraged the nuns with your arrogance and flooded the hallway with bolus — get out Roger before I provide the last sensation you will ever know.'

Roger's stance and expression altered not at all.

'Get out, get *out*!'

'Are you alright, old boy?' asked Roger, pouring himself a drink.

'Get out of here you bloodyminded, oblivious moron!'

'You've lost me, old man,' said Roger, bewildered and amicable.

'I wish to Christ I could,' grated Father, convulsively grasping at a piece of his own head. 'How can I make you understand, Roger — I hate you. I hate you and I want you to go away.'

'Hate me?' Roger smirked. 'Not old Roger Lang.'

'Yes, Roger, hate — we *all* do. I'll *kill* you, Roger — leave *now*.' He started shoving him away, at which Roger was affably perplexed. Father was on the edge of sobbing. 'Get *out*, Roger!'

'Something up, old boy?'

'Get out you bastard!'

Roger frowned and shrugged with a faintly amused incomprehension.

'Get *out*, get *out*!' choked Father, slugging Roger in the gut and feeling progressively feebler and less effective. Roger sipped his drink and raised his eyebrows.

Four hours later, Roger had been baited as far as the front doorway, in which he stood gazing mildly at the grounds. 'Lawn could do with a burn, old fellow,' he remarked, gesturing with his glass. Father was trying to wedge him out with a plank of wood. Roger stood like a rock as Father pushed at his back, legs treddling as though on an exercise bike. Father fired an Elizabethan cannonball which shuttle-gloved upward from the curvature of Roger's arse-groove and paused momentarily in mid-air before dropping through the stairs like a meteorite. Finally Father, Snapper and poor Mr Cannon ran the length of the hallway with a battering ram the inner rings of which indicated an age of a hundred-and-twenty years.

Late in the afternoon, me and Adrienne heard the snarling of a tractor and peered out from her high sanctuary window. Father was perched stern and resolved as he trundled forward, bulldozing Roger across the lawn with a haystack-lift. As they disappeared through the gate Roger was chatting, sipping delicately from a port glass and hailing the heavens with inaudible laughter.

CORTEXKISS

I couldn't believe how long it took everyone to realise Adrienne and me were fucking each other senseless. We'd read about it and now we were doing it, full of mad humour and high spirits. I thought of her anxiously and often, while outwardly appearing to stand idle. I loved her to the very bones in her hair. Talking in glances like identical twins, we drew the scowling attention of Uncle Snapper, who bellowed the observation that Adrienne was 'a wayward, gamine bitch, smiling with her mouth open and clearly up to no bloody good'. Father remarked that a bit of conspiratorial grinning was only to be expected, but Snapper could only repeat that we'd enough casual insolence to choke a pig. 'You're not the first to be bohemian,' Snapper snarled at Adrienne. 'I once played a cello on a deserted beach.'

'I'm sure it was deserted. Instantly.'

Striding this Freudian minefield — a refreshing change from that of my own philosophy — I felt like a Wonderland explorer. Adrienne's blurred face, sick with solemn beauty, floated through large daydreams. At night we were going at it like knives and enjoying long, fluorescent conversations about our migraine experiences. In her company I found myself uniquely awake, my mouth as dry as a biro. The excruciating bliss of her blotting kisses and sensurround legs left me feeling grand and disorderly. At our occasional resolutions to stay away the gods looked down and laughed. 'Did you know a semi-permeable membrane can sometimes be only one molecule thick?' she once asked as we watched a nectar sunset.

'Nothing surprises me anymore.'

Adrienne was writing a book about irony fractals and what drew out the process was her resolve to sample the text from dreams. I had occasional lucid dreams myself but the skill seemed embroidered into Adrienne's DNA. She could stop a dream in its tracks and alter its course simply by acknowledging that she was in fact asleep. Within her dreamworld she frequented a bookshop which was full of works that had never been written in the real world. I told her that if she could transcribe one of these volumes the copyright would belong to her — but she could only keep the shop's image solid for minutes at a time and make a note of a few odd sentences. These she would haul back like interplanetary trophies.

Adrienne's dreaming practice occurred in a hammock strung across a corner of her attic sanctuary. This half of the attic was furthest from the nuns' foundry and thus the quietest part of the Hall. I would lay on the bed watching her drift offworld, floating until the stars disappeared. One evening I gave her a spiral slave-bracelet which the nuns had hammered and engraved for me:

If the sun which lights your eyes
Were thirty-seven times its size
Then you, and I, and all the world
Would start to twitch and fry.

'Laughing boy,' she said, twisting it onto her arm like a screw-thread, 'underneath that curt exterior is a bony latticework brimming with gore.'

She was the first to have said it, and my heart opened like a century flower. I wanted to do more. Adrienne had described her lucid bookshop to me and one night while asleep I found myself there. The proprietor was exactly as she had described him — a moron. I scanned the spine-titles, none of which named an author: *Western Edible Elephants*, *Don't Prophecy in the Corner*, *Exhaustion and the Breast*, *My Pet Git*. The last one seemed to be about some charmer who goes around blowing his nose on other people's shoulders, then says 'You know what this represents? Migration.'

I found a copy of the book from which Adrienne cribbed. It was called *He murdered because he's a murderer because he murdered because he's a murderer because he murdered because he's a murderer because he murdered* ...

Rather than memorise anything I scribbled on the title page, 'We are all god's children, whether he likes it or not.' I've since learned that schoolkids often pass secret notes to eachother in class, so maybe I wasn't so unusual after all.

Meanwhile our experiments continued. My sinuses drained spontaneously when I considered the options available. I daresay we were more noisy than efficient — one night we were surprised in the act and froze like burglars in an arc light. Almost everyone stood in the doorway. 'Bare-faced lust,' Snapper gasped, pop-eyed.

Adrienne grabbed at her trousers, pulling them on. The sanctuary was so thoroughly hexed that nobody could pass the threshold but this didn't keep out the yelling. 'Your depravity confuses the senses and boggles the mind!' hollered the Verger.

'Hang about,' I blurted. 'I mean don't vault to conclusions — it's clear you believe we've no other motive than the spinal joys of effrontery.'

'The sheer, staggering verve of the boy! Gormless and bewildered at the failure of his translucent fibs!'

'The sulphurous swamp of his lust.'

'In for a penny.'

'Did you hear that? I'm bowled over by this I must say.'

'Bedclothes puffing like a grounded parachute.'

'The girl's using him to practise on.'

'I knew it since you were three,' said Snapper. 'Whipping dolls with a jump lead. And you, Adrienne — why can't you snog horses like a normal girl?'

'For fear of catching your germs,' said Adrienne, her voice devoid of all emphasis.

Snapper made to storm into the room and found himself on the landing going the other way.

'I assure you,' said Adrienne tucking in her T-shirt, 'we'll laugh about this later — with the appropriate medication.' She crossed the room with her lithe, swinging stride, and slammed the door on them.

'Well,' I muttered at the window, gazing up at the murky sky, 'said.'

The inquisition followed breakfast. We had seasoned the meal with a sparky fatalism, meeting eachother's glances with a solemn and flirtatious remorse. When the family surrounded us our hearts were less than usually disarmed by the powerful emotions which the Hall's erstwhile fare bestirred.

'Born with an iron spoon in your gob, both of you,' said Father reluctantly, Snapper standing sternly by. 'And you select this as the fine way.'

'We'd do the same again,' said I.

'But quieter,' said Adrienne.

'So that's the song is it?' shouted Snapper, unable to hold back. 'I ought to feed you leg-first to the bloody piano! Take a diamond-drill to your windpipe!'

'So should I,' said Leap. 'How do you like *them* apples?'

'I find them strangely familiar,' I said. 'Like a stainless steel doughnut.'

'Is that the best your beestung brain can come up with?' yelled Snapper. 'Why didn't you drown him at the pump, brother?'

'Changelings,' the Verger bellowed. 'Spooky as hell. The boy there, drooping around like a Shelleyan orphan. Beckoned me into the hot-house. Showed me a skull. I was out of there as fast as my arms and legs could take me.'

'Changelings?' said Adrienne, standing. 'Then we're not your responsibility. Come on, laughing boy, we don't belong here.'

'Time enough to grin when you're coffin-bound and skinless!' shrieked the Verger at our retreating backs. 'Lust is flesh-deep! You can't cheat death — it must be done fair and square!'

'We're all god's children,' whispered Adrienne, nudging me with a hip. 'Whether he likes it or not.'

POD

I ascended the narrow stairwell to the tower where the Verger lurked in a kind of chaotic apothecary. He was writing at a rolltop desk and facing away from me when I entered with a doorcreak. Lambent sunlight played through dust and glass vessels.

'Hello Verger. Weather's brightened up.'

'I'll be the judge of that, laughing boy,' he said without taking his eyes from his work.

I scuffed aimlessly. 'What are you doing?'

'Nothing of interest to the lustful.'

I pottered around the room, trailing a finger through shelfdust and scrutinising murky jars. 'I say, Verger — is this a dove you've preserved?'

The Verger turned, raised his eyebrows and stood enraged, storming over. 'No business of yours, hell-child,' he thundered, yanking at the jar with such force that it flew over his shoulder and exploded against a wall.

The Verger roared me down the stairs to Father's study. 'Bottomless arrogance,' he told him. 'Uncontrollable urges. Smirking evil.'

'In English, Verger.'

'Well there was I in the precious sanctuary of the tower when laughing boy here pranced in and made a remark. A remark which left nothing to the imagination.'

'Listen to me, Verger,' I said, 'the amount of bullshit I take from you is unbelievable. You and your bland assumptions can wade into the lake. If there's one thing I deplore, Father, it's a bigot on the high ground.'

'Have you two fellows ever heard of conciliation?'

The Verger and me began to laugh simultaneously, and halted glowering at each other.

'My point is this,' Father stated mildly. 'Man stands alone in sickness unto death. You could save alot of time, emotion and money by cultivating your own amusement — tying snakes in a knot, pronging your nose with a hoof spike and so on.'

All this was completely alien to the Verger, who regarded Father with tortured amazement. 'Did I hear correctly?'

Father gave me a helpless look. 'I've done what I can.'

'This beggars belief,' said the Verger in astonishment. 'Your son rides roughshod over my life and you sit there like a barrel.'

'What precisely did he do, Verger? Answer without lying if you can.'

'He picked up a jar,' stated the Verger with an effort of self-control, 'and threw it.'

'Threw it?'

'Further than was either pleasant or necessary.'

'Father, do you think I've no more pressing business than to play volleyball with this moron's jars of snot?'

'Is this true, Verger?'

'Why should I put snot of all things in a jar?'

'Postponement of a more permanent decision?'

'A reluctance to accept the natural order,' I suggested. 'After all, Father, you and I try to escape our snot as fast as we can. This gentleman surrounds himself with the stuff.'

'The boy's reasoning is sound, Verger, though I say it with tears in my eyes.'

'I see no tears.'

'All in good time,' said Father. 'You may anticipate a veritable flood.'

'I've better things to do than stand here anticipating *your* secretions!' yelled the Verger, and slammed from the room.

'Did you hear *that*?' I said to Father, with meaning. Ofcourse I hadn't the faintest idea what was in the Verger's jars but I was damned if I'd let him steal the show with lies inferior to my own.

One night when the household was performing a ritual in the reading room, I snuck into the tower with a torch. I swept the beam along the shelves and selected a good-sized jar labelled *V5*, taking it down and unscrewing the lid. Shining the torch inside, all I could see was a murky green sludge. I rocked the jar a little. A pale object emerged through the surface and disappeared again. Impatient, I took down a larger jar. *V9*. I found a pair of tongs and dipped for the contents, bringing out something which looked like a severed tap root, covered in slime. As the slime drooled away I discerned rudimentary features carved into the mould, incredibly ghoulish in the torchlight. I took this as confirmation that the Verger was a member of the clergy.

A creepy feeling was crawling over my shoulders as I shifted a container the size of a larder keg and removed the lid. A soft doll rested inside, half-submerged in liquid.

Flashing the torch around, I could see traces of the Verger's sombre expression in its face. I dropped the torch, and daren't reach in to fish it out.

Stumbling in the darkness I crashed through something, grabbing out for a handhold — the surface in front of me gave onto an unknown space. The Hall was wormholed with hidden anterooms, the blueprints resembling a Mandelbrot fractal. This one was narrow and carpeted with warm earth. Something glinted in the darkness.

This was not a horror movie — I reached out and switched on the light. A large glass vat stood before me. Emerging from a fog of sediment was a fish-eyed Verger, frilled with drifting, ragged mycelium. The cowl had begun to emerge from its head, darkening and hooding over. Here was the last in a series of experimental, trial-run Vergers, each more complete and distinct than the last.

'You've done it now, laughing boy,' boomed a voice behind me.

'Verger,' I stammered, spinning to face him. 'Why aren't you with the others?'

The Verger cast a wily eye at the pupa floating in the tank. '*That*'s why. Don't worry, boy, I won't bite.'

I hadn't known this was among the options.

'Seat yourself on this pile of rats, boy, and I'll explain everything — we've a very limited time.'

I sat down and glanced at the glass vat — the contents moved a slow arm and I heard a faint *clink*.

'Well it's the old, old story,' the Verger began. 'As you know, people generally delegate any real achievement to their offspring and so little is achieved in any one generation. Add to this the contamination of a million opinions it's a wonder anyone does anything by their own impulse. Me and the line were devised to speed up the process unaffected by human concerns. All this cloak and scowl nonsense is just a bit of pretending, the simplest camouflage. We're grown out of spores.'

'I must say Verger you seem remarkably light-hearted about all this.'

'D'you take a dim view?'

'Well I don't know. I don't know, Verger, it's alot to absorb — I mean you tell me you're grown in a jar and then expect me to chuckle or something? Yes I suppose I do take a dim view. I won't sleep soundly for weeks after this.'

'It's a shame, it really is.'

'So when did this nightmare kick off? Who grew those jammy monsters out there?'

'The prototypes? The real Verger — a hundred and fourteen years ago. Keen gardener. Here's one of his botanical sketches, if you're interested.'

He unrolled a scroll which portrayed the Verger's head emerging from the gilled stipe of a bark fungus.

'What sort of life span are we discussing?' I asked, scrutinising the sketch.

'Three months. Enough to outlive human curiosity but being inconspicuous isn't all. The entire three months are spent seeding and growing the next Verger. Delegation again, you see. We all record and write instructions but it seems personal wisdom can only be learnt in the physical, not passively from a book. Each generation is as moronic as the last, a clean slate. Almost no cumulative knowledge.' He smiled. His face imploded like a blown egg, releasing a little puff of dust. 'Sorry you had to see this, laughing boy,' he said through the mess of his face, then with a loud snap he collapsed like an articulated skeleton.

I prodded the still mass at my feet — it rustled like a sack of leaves. *Enjoy your childhood*, I thought, *while you can.*

The vat began to bubble and bump like an eggboiler. The new Verger was shifting its limbs in the swirling suspension, slow and blind. The plasma roiled as the creature reached a glistening hand over the edge of the tank. There was no lid. The new head arose from behind the glass. The film across its milky eyes broke and it blinked at me. The caul over its mouth tore as the new Verger tried to speak. 'Oh,' it said.

'Eh, Verger?' I asked, unwrapping a new stick of gum.

The Verger squinted like a newborn. 'Oh,' he said, 'what a tangled web we weave.'

DEMOLITION

'What do you mean by bringing this dog in here?' rumbled Uncle Snapper with a compressed anger or perhaps fear, as Father entered followed by the skittering spaniel Nelson. The dog sat down, raised its eyebrows and regarded Snapper in a sarcastic pretence at wounded surprise.

It was pointless to pretend that Nelson was a normal hound. He was in the habit of smiling, laughing or performing abrupt and eccentric dances. He would begin a sentence and stop as everyone turned. He sat upright in an armchair and read the morning paper, snapping it open and seeming to understand. He signalled the answers to complex arithmetical questions by biting Uncle Snapper to the appropriate count. Father stated that dogs like Nelson were part of life's rich tapestry and Snapper remarked that if he spotted a dog like Nelson in a tapestry he'd publicly eat pure lard.

Anyway it all came to a head one afternoon when Snapper bounded up on both legs claiming that Nelson, who was sat nearby like a loaf of bread, had accused him of being a royalist.

'This has gone far enough,' shouted Professor Leap, and pointed at Nelson. 'The number of delusions you've projected onto that poor hound it's a wonder he hasn't ignited like kindling under a laser. *I*'ll tell you how to prove whether this tormented animal speaks or not.'

Leap came up with the notion of attaching a voice-activated dictaphone to Nelson's collar. If the mammal made a remark we would have proof positive of this phenomenon. Leap went ahead with the procedure and after a while the machine was removed and the results replayed as the household gathered to listen in sharp-eared and anxious silence. The recording began mundanely enough:

SNAPPER (*shouting*): Didn't I tell you at fantastic expense I don't care a straw for your opinions?

THE VERGER (*shouting*): And I know you're a cocky, arrogant liar!

SNAPPER (*shouting*): You dare say that to my face?

THE VERGER (*shouting*): That's where your ears and brain are housed unless I'm sadly mistaken!

FATHER (*shouting*): Not the drill, brother!

SNAPPER (*shouting*): I'll kill him!

FATHER (*shouting*): Grab him, Cannon!

POOR MR CANNON (*shouting*): I'll be dragged apart by lions before I'll offer help (*incoherent*) obliterate all reason and kill (*possibly 'everyone'*) each and every chance I get! All matter is localised in (*sobs, a shriek*)

SNAPPER (*shouting*): Get that bloody dog out of here!

FATHER (*shouting*): Snapper's gone berserk, Cannon — put the dog out!

Amid further domesticities the back door was heard to slam, and here the tape took an unexpected turn. An unfamiliar voice was speaking, with only the peaceful hiss of trees as a background. The voice was almost inaudible, like a tiny child whispering into someone else's ear. We strained to discern the words:

'Once again I sit like an exhausted pimp at the doors of a Tangier whorehouse. How can these fools be used or forgiven. They laugh as everything of value is blasted beyond repair. Flinging objects and wasting my precious time. The so-called master and mistress — what a sham of a marriage. He at his drawingboard, dreading the hour she will slam out a meal from which all distinguishing marks have been removed. A chewed gauntlet, a challenge — identify this if you can. And he, an apparently sophisticated man, secretly eats wood to assuage his hunger. So ofcourse reason becomes a guilt-laced and occasional luxury. Leap has his skeleton professionally sharpened. Weeps with the aid of a stencil. Lack of emotion given the terms and prestige of science. Squeezes the world's heart through his fingers like a flan. Knows as well as I do history's a balloon-folder provoking jeers from the peanut gallery. Money's elsewhere. Eye to the main chance. Eagerness personified. Rat up a drainpipe. Even when he thinks, he's lying. Poor Mr Cannon — reckless dolt. Dares show his face in the village. Helix of social obligations. Bellows in the bar. Salty anecdotes concerning past embarrassments. Gored by a bull while standing aloof. Caught carmine-faced at bizarre crimes. Drinks like a king. Says he's had enough when he crunches glass. Faces dawn like the Turin Shroud. Zinc-eyed in a ditch. Meek as a clubbed seal. Snapper though — there's a fierce one. Man on a mission. Shaves with a blowlamp. Name's a rash across the dynamite records. Ignorance run like a well-drilled army. Masturbates eleven times a day.'

Snapper went berserk and was wrestled immediately into a headlock. Adrienne was being discussed:

'... playing Ophelia but on the quiet she manacles laughing boy to the bed and rides on his blank face — these so-called children are a mutant anomaly. There's never been anything to stop laughing boy. It's a tragedy he was ever allowed to take in the worldly snorkel of his thumb. His only speck of hope for salvation is embedded in the missing and hopelessly untraceable nose-tip of the Nile Sphinx. Nanny Jack — malevolently unresponsive. Paralysed on one side, boring on the other. No ambiguity there. The Verger. No more human than I am. Smoke inhabits his trousers. Very occasionally he opens his rolltop desk and releases a creature for exercise — a live trilobyte the size of a telephone. Fiddles its legs in the dim light. The only thing capable of making the Verger laugh. Think about that. Burst — total dementia. Miracle he's upright. Only man I know who can strut and whimper at the same time. Danger to himself and others. Corners children. Sinister and panting. Toothful grimace. Reads Wordsworth. Say no more. This place — a triumph over logic and syntax, funded by fraud and the threat of violence. Gargoyles screaming obscenities. God have mercy on us all.'

There was a brief pause, the sound of a door, and we were back in the kitchen:

THE VERGER (*shouting*): — wraps his gun in cashmere!
SNAPPER (*shouting*): I'll kill you!
FATHER (*shouting*): Grab his legs, Cannon!
POOR MR CANNON (*shouting*): Minister for trade (*inaudible*) face like a trout (*crashing noises*) retribution —

Father pressed the off-button calmly. 'Well there you have it, gentlemen — food for thought.'

'Food for thought you bastard?' said Snapper, incredulous. 'It was the dog — talking. D'you propose to stand there pretending otherwise?'

'All I heard was an unfamiliar voice giving the game away. Could have been any one of us, playing the fool.'

'I recall that conversation,' stated the Verger, 'regarding Snap's garbage-ridden existence. Poor Mr Cannon shoved the dog out but did not close the door correctly. Moments later Nelson re-entered and began staring again. These are the facts.'

'Laughing boy's window,' Leap announced, looking me in the eye, 'is directly above the kitchen door.'

'*Laughing boy!*' bellowed Snapper, grabbing me.

After five hours of futile denial, I was left tied to a tree near the lake. 'Think on the anguish and trouble your childish trick has caused,' ordered Leap as they departed. Standing there alone, all I could think of was how much I needed Adrienne to sit on my face. I had indeed been at my window when Nelson was standing below. I had whispered nothing, but had heard it all.

Now Nelson skittered over and took up a post a short distance away, watching my struggles and smiling in resolute silence.

It was the longest afternoon of my life.

HOSPITALITY

Colour in reverse, Lord Brakes and Lady Marjoram were like something grown in an ashtray. Next to them Roger Lang resembled a fascinating individual. Algernon Brakes pressed his eyebrows nightly in a copy of *The Pickwick Papers*. Even his aura was made of tweed. Lady Marjoram seemed unaware that her gloves were removable and appeared to be wearing a marquee. As welcome as a vase on a butcher's slab, their very shadow inspired in us all a valiant disgust.

They insisted on visiting us as though they were neighbours and perhaps they were. With admirable restraint we responded to their knock by ducking under the windows and if they entered we hid as best we could. Brakes and Marjoram would wait for hours in the kitchen under the deep ticking of the clock, or staring blankly up at Ramone the moose-head, over whom we had long since pushed a bucket of cement which had dried to form a permanent nosebag. Trudging subdued through the silent house, the pair would peer through doorways and then give eachother vacant looks. A visit to the storage attic was spent tearing through giant webs, crashing into disconcertingly lifelike marionettes and so on.

On one regrettable occasion, however, they abruptly opened the cupboard in which Father and I were silently standing. 'Er — Brakes old fellow,' said Father briskly, 'you've met the lad. Laughing boy — you know Algie.'

'I have had the pleasure of scraping some from a bucket.'

'You'll be forgiven for thinking my son here is a disciple of Satan. He's just a small boy adjusting to the mayhem and corruption of circumstance. Shall we adjourn to the sitting room?'

As the guests started off in that direction Father ran the other way, his face a carnival of luck and mischief.

After several moments Brakes and Marjoram re-emerged from the sitting room to find me stood in the hallway alone. 'Father finds you drab,' I stated, 'and has run away. It falls to me to entertain you. Come here.' The guests hesitated, looking fretfully at each other.

'Do not be concerned,' I said, any pretence at interest cold and dead. 'We are composed largely of water. This way.'

Leading them into the kitchen, I motioned for them to sit down and stood near the progressive wall markings which, on days of family togetherness, Father would pencil up to record my pain threshold. 'I spy,' I muttered, 'with my little eye. Something beginning with death.'

Brakes and Marjoram fired startled glances at eachother and their surroundings.

'Death-mask,' I intoned, opening the larder to reveal that of Lenin. I went to the door. 'Consider this your home. There's the kettle. Tip out the scorpion. Goodnight.'

Crowded into the boiler room, everyone sat around on

bales of Father's funny money. Overlit by a bare lightbulb, Snapper resembled a bottlenose dolphin. 'Well laughing boy?' he whispered fiercely. 'Are they gone?'

'No,' I hissed. 'They're in the kitchen, trying to decide.'

'This is ridiculous,' said Snapper. 'Hiding underground to avoid the dullards.'

'Study history,' muttered Leap.

'Go and talk to them, boy,' frowned Father. 'Make them understand this isn't the time or the place.'

I entered the kitchen with a strangled cry — Brakes and Marjoram awoke in alarm, blinking. They had been resting their heads on the table. 'The sleep of the innocent,' I sneered. 'You do not perceive the anguish you are causing here. The mean trick you are playing. Don't look at me that way. I wouldn't give a pinch of dust what you think of me, but there is far more at stake.'

Lord Brakes and Lady Marjoram gaped blearily in the stark light as I explained morphic resonance. 'Theoretically if I throttle a mime on one side of the world, people on the other side will spontaneously get the same idea. Mime-strangling is not the best example, being by no means a new or original impulse.' I discussed the hundredth monkey principle. 'When I strangle that monkey,' I said emphatically, 'it *stays* dead.'

Brakes opened his mouth, closed it without having said anything, and cleared his throat.

'Well?' Snapper scowled as I entered the basement. 'Have they pushed off at last?'

'They are still in the kitchen,' I stated mournfully.

Snapper was agitated. 'By god, brother,' he rumbled to Father. 'The boy should be fed his own jaw.'

'Pay no attention,' Father soothed me. 'Your uncle's pills

are in the treehouse. Nobody's going to feed you a jaw.'

'We must frighten them away,' said Leap, nodding. 'It is the only way to be rid of these soporific guests.'

I floated into the kitchen dressed as the Grim Reaper. For this I had borrowed Nan's scythe and robe. In fact to all intents and purposes I floated into the kitchen dressed as Nan but I thought this would be enough. Lord Brakes and Lady Marjoram appeared to have prepared a small meal and they looked up from this as I shouted a few remarks on the subject of doom. 'Decay,' I suggested. 'Decay — and don't contradict me.'

Brakes and Marjoram crunched toast, spectating my performance with a mild curiosity.

'It's no good,' I said in the steam room, throwing down the scythe. 'They're morons — don't even grasp the concept of peril.'

'What we need,' said Leap, 'is something that'll have adrenalin spurting out of their ears. A first-class haunting. Aren't we directly below the kitchen?'

Within minutes we had set up a fiendish choir of wailing cries which would echo upward through the floor and cause Brakes and Marjoram to consider phantoms a distinct possibility. Amid the ullulating shrieks of Father, Snapper, Leap and myself, the Verger drummed on a variety of kegs and recited creepy Latin in a low gurgle. Adrienne screamed as though beautifully deranged. In his element, poor Mr Cannon shuddered to beat the band, releasing strained belches and punching himself in the face. Uncle Burst repeatedly whooped some sort of nonsense about having spiderwebs for nerve tissue. Under the swinging lightbulb, Nanny Jack sat silent as the grave. We hurled forged notes, choking eachother and yelping oddly amid fluttering cash. One of the kegs exploded, flooding the basement with blue ink. Snapper began to howl at the ceiling, his face stretched and demented. Others took up the cry, tearing at their garments.

The turbulent display had an audience of two. Unnoticed in a corner, Lord Brakes and Lady Marjoram looked on, the very souls of patience.

HA BLOODY HA

Poor Mr Cannon strained under the tyranny of an oafish, misplaced merriment. He was everything I wanted to be — consistent, Japanese, heavy-set as a Bassett hound. His clothing spoke of chance and chaos. A marble-eyed wreck, snorting creosote and swaying like a metronome, he would arrive at the doorstep wearing a boiled shirt and the crooked smile of a snowman. For a few bob he'd explain his truncated morality, which consisted of his whispering 'You are free to go' repeatedly into your ear.

Having awoken in one too many fountains, Cannon boasted that when it came to being harmless he was a Triton among the minnows and, vowing to prove it once and for all, embarked upon a campaign of insensibility and disquiet in the village. In a mainburst of sarcasm and open mimicry he stood in the square reciting a litany of unsettling dogma and punching his ears with a staple gun. He tipped a mess of eels from a diplomatic bag, headbutted parked cars and conspicuously fainted. Concerned citizens approached his prone form and his eyes sprang open, staring like those of a new corpse. He slammed his face unexpectedly against nocturnal windows and stayed there, as sinister and inconvenient as a fiend. Walking as carefully as a rod puppet to the sound of a moody snare drum, he talked about trolls with a studied nonchalance until he was swept from the scene by a flying wedge of cops in riot gear.

Five years later he stood before an undead judge. He could barely recall the events in question and neither could anyone else. But the judge was proud of his pea-green grasp of history. His heart had dried and rattled inside him like a blown yolk.

I can only work from others' reports as at the time I was making a study of different kinds of fern and taking them back to my room at the Hall where I pasted them onto a tin effigy of a snarling midget. Those were the days when a man could really accomplish something, if he had a will to.

But by all accounts everyone rallied in this rare instance of our mindful community meeting the monotone. Cannon kept annoying the judge by pleading 'gilly' and the character witnesses, far from being a balm, poured oil on the bonfire of Cannon's ordeal. His troubles brought out the best in everyone.

Professor Leap was a smart one, having asked the nuns to make him a tie of hammered steel. Standing stern and mannered in the dock, he ignored everyone. The judge was forced to address him directly. 'Mr Leap, is it? In your experience is the defendant a violent man?'

'God, no. Never fitted in. Recall a time he entered gingerly with a gun at the waist. Pitiful as a wasp in a coffin. His scorn terrifies me more than any assault. Every day we are brushed by the damaged wing of his sanity. Caught him in the hot-house once, snogging a badger. Questioned him. His eyes filmed over with a membrane. Even I know that's not where a membrane's meant to be. I was appalled and fascinated. Climbed a hill. Had to think. The air smelt of distance. A morning of fog and cobwebs. Then, silence was shattered. Cannon — that snail-stamping bastard over there — seeing fit to answer my enquiries through twelve Marshall amplifiers. Feedback like you wouldn't believe. And not a proper answer — not from archangel Cannon here. Flaying torrent of abuse, m'ud, from start to finish. Stuff I couldn't repeat in this hellhole you call a court.'

The judge's dry lips had just begun to unseal when Leap continued, to his stunned consternation.

'Ofcourse a man like me could effortlessly write it down for your appraisal, m'ud. I'm sure you'll understand before too long as to why I felt it important to crush the bones of his throat.' Leap inscribed something on a scrap of paper, moving his mouth and frowning with fierce concentration. Then he looked up brightly, admired his work and handed the note to the usher. 'Keep it under your hat.'

The judge put on his glasses, examined the note and instantly tore his glasses off again, gazing slack-faced at Leap. The note contained the following information:

> Eddie was a salesman
> He'd soon saw off your legs
> Then charge you twenty smackers
> For wasting his time.

'Is this,' said the judge, brandishing the note, 'all you can provide as a character reference for that man?'

'Yes,' said Leap. 'Though elementary prudence would demand you drop it like a spider.'

At this point Snapper bounded up and blurted, 'I've never

met this razor-eating moron in my life! And if I had I'd spill gut jelly to conceal the fact!'

The judge registered surprise at Snapper's outburst, and this was enough to break the dam of Snap's resistance. He was carried sobbing from the room with an unnecessary show of turbulence. The rake-marks on the doorframe were caused not by Snapper's hands but his ribcage, which had the tendency to spring closed like a beartrap. 'It's curtains for veracity, lads,' he cried like a bosun announcing a killer storm, and disappeared.

'So what do you say, m'ud, shall we get married or what?' Leap demanded. 'I'm a busy man — d'you think I've a life to live in this sandblasted nipple-ranch?'

The judge was appalled.

'I'm a strong one,' bellowed Leap, 'with a morality as superfluous and cherished as a healthy appendix. I've known my destiny since I grew a fist and became a man.'

'Are you *sick*?' asked the judge, squinting through a blizzard of incredulity.

Leap gave a carefree laugh, then stopped short. 'I've had it up to' — and he vaulted from the stand, shoving through dullards across the chamber to reach the far wall, where he prodded a stubby finger into the eye of a bust of Samuel Johnson — '*here* with your questions! You and your forbidding radiance can't stop me now!' Leap began to prance with a kind of flamboyant scorn, and several startled officials bolted up and tackled him from all sides. Outside in the hallway, Snapper lit a fart of historic magnitude and blew a door into the courtroom in a hail of splinters — a fireball roared across the room and banged open in midair, searing the eyebrows from the front row of the viewers' gallery. Fire extinguishers were discharged, blasting the flames and filling the room with a dense roiling snow.

The surprise witness was Roger Lang, the surprise being that they let him in. 'Cannon,' he said, sipping port. 'Cannon. Name rings a bell. Um. Ah — snogged a badger. That the one? Yes, Cannon. Boon colleague. Salad days. Man of strong views, dignity, and breeding — breeding fast. Bristling egomania and inhuman cries in a slithery vault. Knelt down and punched the soft face of a cat as if he'd been doing it all his life. I confess I'm baffled by my own reactions to the bastard.'

To everyone's horror, Roger would not leave the stand. His jocular reminiscence drifted on as the usher tugged at his arm. He was oblivious to time or indifference. A prospective lifetime of this rubbish crackled before the onlookers like a lake of fire. The port Roger raised was the blood of the lamb. Soon he was clutching the sill as fifteen people tried to pull him away by the legs — stretched horizontal in midair, he was laughing uncontrollably and relating an anecdote. His trousers were dragged off without effect. Someone grabbed the cigar from Roger's mouth and threw it away in impotent rage. 'This trouserless belligerence is putting the frighteners on everyone!' yelled the judge. 'Get out of here, get *out*!'

'Get *out*, Roger,' shouted Snap, and took up an identical sill-clutching, tug-legged position beside him. Soon there were seven people holding onto the stand and the usher resorted to smashing their hands with a gavel. A court sketch of that instant was later dismissed as a madman's dream.

When the Verger was summoned to the stand he rose out of the floor like a rashly invoked phantom. Particles of light were being sucked into the folds of his cloak and extinguished. 'It must be a dark responsibility,' he boomed at the judge. 'Being the first link in the mighty food chain.' A tension filled the room like black molasses. 'Do my eyes deceive me or is this the husk of a useless past. No need to trawl for brazen loudmouths here. The brain is a morsel for medieval crows. The facts are trampled by a blithe torquemada. The venue's crippling banality disgusts me even as I feed upon its evil heart. And to think I hesitated. I envy poor Mr Cannon, this coldly brilliant man in whom sheer implausibility has supplanted emotion. Centre stage. Inverse pandemonium. We are meat puppets, lacking only a script and purpose.'

The Verger's shape rippled ominously, swirling inward at the centre. Reports differ wildly as to what happened next. Some say he imploded, taking half the furniture with him as he reversed out of existence. Some say he became a black smoke which creeped over the walls and ceiling, dropping dead ants upon the assembly. Others report that he simply crawled away on his hands and knees, snickering like an evil barber. A point of accord is that everyone gasped and sucked air when he was gone, realising that they had involuntarily ceased breathing in his presence.

Father took the stand and caught the judge's eye as though with a freshwater rod. 'Truth to the slaughter, eh m'ud?' he smirked, and winked conspiratorially.

'I beg your pardon,' stated the judge, but Father only chuckled as though sharing the oldest and naughtiest joke in the world.

Father was the bigot in a bigot's nightmare — assured, unreachable, unharmed and unharmful. He had many good things to say about Cannon, not least concerning his 'downright, unabashed inertia'. 'Cannon's cheek by flapping jowl with the newly dead,' chortled Father. 'Pathologically recumbent. No telling where he'll faint next. Paint isn't dry on him. Idiot glee. Blathering simpleton. Salt of the Earth — not counting the stuff you can make in a lab. His integrity can be doubted only by a sodomite in exile, m'ud. Even the rooks stop cawing when Cannon here steps out of the house. Roof-rolling high performance cars. Strangling teddybears with piano wire in a room lit like an aquarium. Tripping obnoxious brats. Laughing up other people's sleeves. Spawning havoc. Head crowded with ambivalence. Slaver when I see him approaching. Drag my leg. Anything to frighten that aberration back into the shadows. Locked in an empty aircraft hangar he'd find a mistake to make. Yet I don't pretend to be filled with hay. The folds of my brain are jostling like a crowd viewed from above, m'ud. But I can't think of a time when Cannon hasn't sat whimpering with regret at the results of his bloodyminded mischief. I like to think I'm in reasonable control of my faculties. Let's see you make a joke out of that.'

Father was wearing a rubber mask of his own face beneath which was a rubber mask of poor Mr Cannon. The idea was to whip off the outer mask and pretend to be Cannon to save Cannon the embarrassment of addressing the crowd. But when Father went to tear off the outer mask, he grabbed both in one handful and whipped them away to reveal his own face again. This pointless act went mostly unremarked among the onlookers, who seemed to have become numb to everything. 'Serves us all well,' pronounced Father, standing down, 'for living in a land where it's the same time everywhere and you can't take a step in any direction without kicking into the sea.'

Sporting the herbal trousers he would later champion, Cannon stood in the dock, regarding his surroundings as though from a lost pet poster. He had a surgical torch in his mouth so that every time he spoke the room strobed like a foundry. 'Blood was up,' he said, explaining his forgotten behaviour.

'So was the sun but it has never entered this courtroom,' said the judge, attempting a kind of pre-emptive control over the docile Cannon. 'How did you become such a lethal asset to the forces of slobbering deviance?'

'Not overnight,' said Cannon without guile.

The lifelike brevity of his reply sent the judge scrabbling for paperwork. 'According to this your hobbies are prowling, weeping, casting a sudden reflection upon placid water and exhibiting a cool, calculated cheek. And you once saw fit to drop a snake upon a passing shepherd.'

'A subdued-looking fish, m'ud.'

Resilient in the face of honesty, the judge answered with a laconic snort.

'I'm not one to blow my own trumpet, but — ' Cannon began parping expertly on a small trumpet which the usher swiped immediately away from him. As a fallback measure Cannon was wearing a rubber mask of his own face beneath which was a rubber mask of Father — both of these came away with the trumpet, flapping like dishgloves. Cannon grabbed his shirt and tore it with a convulsive shriek.

'Why have you rent your clothes?' asked the judge wearily.

'Because I didn't want to rip my own.'

The judge embarked upon such a grim and lengthy stare that several people thought him dead and began to scream. During this diversion Father snatched Cannon's masks from the floor and put them on, resembling Cannon for a split second before standing and ripping off the outer one with a yell which caught everyone's attention. Wearing a mask of his own face, he was simply standing there like a ringmaster in rehearsal. Realising his mistake, he tore off the second mask to reveal his own face beneath. 'What is this fathomless horseplay?' the judge demanded. 'I can't tell what this mazurka of connivance and evasion tempts me to feel.' He looked coldly at Cannon.

There was anxiety among the Hall residents as it seemed on the cards that Cannon would cheerfully tear off his own face to show he had nothing to hide. 'Guilty,' the judge sneered at last. Cannon did not react immediately, thinking that he himself had said it. But upon realising that he had been condemned and that his ordeal was over, he let flow tears of laughter and relief. The judge became indignant, raising the sentence to his tumbleweed heart's content. At this point Uncle Burst happened to stick his finger into an electrical socket, draining the local grid into the inland sea of his ego. The room became a darkness in which the multiphonic screams of the startled were the only entertainment.

A single high-frequency shriek rang out as the lights went up. The judge's mask had been removed to reveal a tense mess of bone and meat like red melted wax — it was a royal portrait of bitterness and misspent hatred. His pain seemed honest.

Poor Mr Cannon stood as innocent as you or I, leaning on the dock ledge and gazing skyward like a rococo cherub.

ENVY OF THE WORLD

Besides formation belching the main activity which constituted quality time at the Hall was the pretence at being dead. Ofcourse there was Harbinger Night, during which the entire household rushed up to the reading room and rolled strangely along the walls, a tradition I always took for granted. But that was only once a year — we pretended to be dead all the time.

We were experts at vacant immobility. Whole days were passed tilted dummy-like at the table, cod-eyed and agape. I've recently unearthed a family portrait in which we are grouped staring past the camera, slack and departed. When visiting the seaside we would collar a brisk passerby to snap the family and drop abruptly dead as we were brought into focus, provoking a kind of anguished scream from the traumatised bystander. We spent entire afternoons lying dead in the surf, rolled by the waves, our limbs flaccid as the ocean raised us and put us gently down. In England death is a way of being left alone. Even clowns or barbers will reserve respect for the departed. I have known meddlesome clerics to run snivelling the moment I collapse.

Executives roar off in open-top cars. Street-mimes shuffle awkwardly, ducking into taxis and peering white-faced from the rear window. Horses look away in bored disdain. Policemen fail to notice. In other lands the flight of the spirit is an end to privacy — here it's a start.

Adrienne once played dead as far as the morgue. She opened her eyes and swung off the slab, padding through the chill chamber. There were several other bodies in the vault, and these too opened their eyes expecting a time alone and free. There was some embarrassed laughter at the realisation, and then a heavy, imploding silence. Lie back and think of England.

THE PICTURE OF UNCLE SNAP

Adrienne had painted a portrait of Uncle Snap sitting bolt upright next to a gremlin in a strange, drab room. Though small, the picture was incredibly compelling. Its high resolution had so much hold on the hallway we found ourselves gathering in front of it to fight. After a couple of years it became a centre of gravity for every punch-up we had. More than once I was caught trying to peer past the frame to see more of the room inside. Adrienne wouldn't say how she'd done it and Snapper himself pretended not to care.

Strangest of all was the slow transformation which Snapper's painted image seemed to be undergoing. The facial expression appeared progressively more relaxed and lighthearted while in actual life he grew increasingly angry. One morning we found the painted Snapper beaming like a cherub, its eyes filled with love — Father visited the treehouse and interrupted him frantically wedging the restrainer panel from a submachine gun. 'Full auto, brother!' shrieked Snap. 'Think of the damage I could do with that!' And he barrelled headfirst across the room, missing Father by a mere three yards and flying through the open door. Breaking his right arm in the fall, he became increasingly enraged. Yet over the next few weeks there was no change in the picture, and this set me thinking.

Climbing into the treehouse, I engangled him in light conversation and hunted for signs of creativity. All I found was a brass rubbing of his ego. 'Listen Snap,' I shouted, 'I know only a freak in a hurry could mistake you for an innovator but don't you think it's strange that your stupid expression changes all the time in that bloody portrait?'

Snapper stood and charged headfirst in the wrong direction, flying through the open door.

When Snap was recovered I began a nightly vigil of the picture. The changes always occurred at night and I was determined to see them happen. There was alot of nodding off and rushing over to see if I'd missed anything. Nothing changed. Until one night I was checking out the picture in the light of a torch.

The little gremlin which sat in its own chair next to Snapper, its face full of mischief. The bare board floor coated in grey ash. Dim, pastiche wallpaper and ill darkness. Creepy, indistinct corners.

I realised I was inside looking out at the dark hallway. The seat and everything was attached to me and nothing but my eyes could move. Straining to see through the visor of my face, I located the figure seated next to me. It was all front, like a piece of stage scenery. I was in a sterile, airless, annihilative space. It was starkly scary — my spine was an electric eel, stinging itself and wanting out. The whole setup was familiar. The moment I thought to scream the

Snap figure said: 'I increasingly think action is the only way.' Its voice was like ice and vinegar.

'I didn't burn the nerve farm,' I said, uncertain. 'It was Snapper. Doesn't like people pushing the envelope.'

'Pretends he doesn't,' answered Mister Hieronymus. 'On the quiet he drags out a vein and uses it as a skipping rope. Eyes front, laughing boy, if you want the facts.'

I looked into the hallway — Snapper walked up in his pyjamas, brandishing a fine art brush. He reached up and carefully retouched the Snap figure's face, drawing up the mouth into an inane smile, smoothing out the brow. His eyes strange and glassy, he turned and plodded off.

'Sleepwalking,' said Mister Hieronymus. 'Subconscious urges he'd never admit to.'

'Why did you stand for that?' I asked, looking askance at the wet face of the Snapper effigy.

'I've taken the opportunity to inhabit this nightmare,' it replied, 'so as I can talk to you — it seems nobody else will. You'll be left alone here, laughing boy. Your life'll fly off its hinges.'

'And I wanted everything to be so perfect.'

'Now's not the hour for snide abstraction, boy — don't imagine I thrive upon perching like something preserved in a museum. Everyone's reading more into this than you are. As sure as you're sitting there, a garden beetle's backflaps will lift to reveal a hotrod engine.'

'I'm not convinced I'm sitting here.'

'Please yourself. You're a Machiavellian bird I'll say that for you.'

'Wasn't he that bastard who said authority was the spice?'

'And more. That by making an example or two a ruler

will prove more compassionate than those who allow riot and disorder.'

'If such examples are proof of compassion then surely disorders will prove the more compassionate as they harm the whole community, while executions only affect individuals.'

'Can't change a circle to a square without reducing its surface area, laughing boy.'

'What about a cube?'

'You mar my argument by no more clever means than an increase in dimensions.'

'To no greater number than that in which normal people move and have their being, Sideshow — it's not my fault your crap argument hasn't the stamina to exist in the real world. This is terrible. Get me out of here.'

I was instantly back in the hallway, gasping for air. My body was aching like inept architecture. In the picture Snap beamed and the little creature beside him was looking, its head now turned aside.

Late the next day I started feeling stupid for bailing out — it was clear Hieronymus had information to impart. I went to the hallway but the picture was gone — Snapper had burnt it. 'The gremlin,' Snapper said, fronting off defensively. 'Suddenly didn't like it. All day wherever I went — felt the little shit was watching me.'

METAL BOX

Like human hair, the reputation of a saint grows after death. Uncle Blute had driven a Morris Traveller into the lake. Now the turquoise square of its roof rippled just below the surface, dappled with emerald moss and jacinth rust. 'Your mother's brother,' stated Snap. 'Strange chap. Eyebrows met in the middle of someone else's face. Insisted the same birds were being born every few years. Finite number. Made calculations. Invented devices he couldn't operate. Disappeared for days at a time. Staggered back unable to tell the tale, covered in insect bites. A gentleman in the days when the word had a meaning.'

Adrienne said she dimly recalled him doing a stunt with his nose. 'Turned it inside out,' she said, frowning. 'So it looked like a sea anemone. Arced over laughing — never grew tired of it.'

'Well he won't be doing anything with his muzzle these days,' I said. 'First thing to go Father says and I'm tempted to agree with him. Becomes a luxury.'

But I was forgetting the lake. Like certain Nevada lakes its water was clinically pure, preserving anything which sank there. After ten years Blute was at the wheel in immaculate condition.

Yet the strangest thing was that due to the water's conductive alkalinity the headlights and radio were still on. If you sat at a particular spot on the shore you could faintly hear the weather report. At night a corner of the lake glowed an agreeably ghoulish green. Adrienne would sit with me on an overhanging rock, her face underlit as she crunched an apple. 'He was ready.'

On the anniversary of his death it was decided we should endure a memorial service for this amusing fellow. We trooped down to the lake in a squelch of rubber insulation, carrying wreaths of iron flowers which the nuns had hammered to order. 'Why the hell are we doing *this* now?' I asked, tugging on Father's sleeve.

He raised his mask. 'Man is made up of body and spirit, but not until death is he forced to take sides.'

That shut me up — I bit upon the snorkel and looked toward the water. The others were already getting in, big ripples spreading — they were like zealots in a ritual cleansing. As I began wading after them I heard classical music throbbing through the water and thought maybe it wasn't such a malignant ceremony. Above all, I was curious to see an authentic gentleman.

As my mask went under the surface everything became luminous. I saw the others floating like haunts around the two headlights. Debussy's *Rondes de printemps* was playing as Mother laid a metal wreath on the bonnet. I couldn't help but marvel at the condition of the wooden panelling.

'There's Blute,' said Father, touching his mask to mine. 'Absolutely mint.'

The driver, whose white balloon head became visible

through the windshield, was certainly in good repair. He was staring like a madman, his chalky hands still on the wheel. His nose was squashed against the glass like the sucker of a snail, nostrils flared. Light and shadow shifted like commune ideologies, giving the illusion of life. But there was no reaction when I laid the wreath — nothing there atall. This was either a dead, abandoned body or a wax mannequin. Neither was of interest to me.

As I stared, the music faded and an announcer began to describe the royal celebrations. It was Jubilee year.

ITCHES IN THE SKY

Snapper missed his medication and started seeing itches in the sky. 'Truth is as small as an itch,' he had said that morning and we should have been alarmed. Now he was utterly incoherent, springing over hedges yelling gibberish which two years later he patiently explained as meaning 'I'd give my weight in snails to know what's going on around here.' He entered the sitting room covered in ferns and wearing a chrome helmet. He was laughing like Lamb at Hazlitt's wedding as he described the web-like constellations of truth and the inevitable collapse and infernal damnation of the universe.

'Informal did he say?' asked Leap.

'Infernal,' said Father, reading the paper.

'I thought he said informal too,' I said cheerfully, stroking a South European wolf spider.

'Ofcourse it'll be in*formal*!' bellowed Snapper, transfigured with rage. He swiped up a chestnut pan and slammed it down on the spider, which now resembled a discarded glove.

'You utter bastard,' I said, staring. I had been training

the spider to form part of an alarm-clock mechanism and everything had been just fine. 'You did that deliberately.'

Snap was hooting with laughter.

'I hope you're proud of yourself,' said Leap. 'After all the boy's work. Those of us who give a damn are of the opinion that you're put together with glue. Ribcage like a mantrap. This resentful malice of yours. Perhaps I shouldn't mention it at this point but when viewed through an obverse gravitational lens you appear to have the face of a king prawn.'

'I know it but what about the droog?' shouted Snapper, pointing at me. 'His pockets are full of tiny bones!'

'Nonsense,' I said quickly.

'Oh yes, brother,' shouted Snap. 'It's incredibly obvious. And I'm disappointed you found it necessary to produce such truculent and abrasive offspring.'

'Oh I don't know,' said Father with an air of judicious consideration. 'Sheets stretch in transformation, a new creature brims a little amid its claws — doesn't matter in the long run.'

'Are you quite *sure* it doesn't?' asked Leap, tortuously aghast, and turned to look at me with a new and appalled understanding.

'I'm completely informed about everything,' Snapper was saying imperatively, 'and the beauty of it is I'm reluctant to share.' He went on at length about badgers and hope, concluding with the statement that he'd scribble down certain metaphysical truths and gloat over them privately till the cows came home. 'Meanwhile the lot of you will fade and die,' he said and, hollering with laughter, bounded from the room.

Two days later he sat up in bed and clutched his temples.

'Have I been stroked with a bone saw?' he asked.

'Snap?' said Father, looking in. 'Up at last. Lost your marbles, brother. Been pointing at Caesar for three days. Talking about the facts.'

'I remember now — or some of it. Thought I was ill and sat here idle for half a lifetime. Kicking through grapes to the lavatory. Even read *Five Weeks in a Balloon*.'

'That was just yesterday, brother. Before that you were padlocking birds to branches. Sat naked playing a bassoon. Went to bat for the big issues.'

'Doesn't sound like me. Didn't shoot anyone?'

'Not a soul, brother — strangest part of the whole affair. How you feeling?'

'Like a dog in amber,' Snapper croaked. 'And what's all this about the facts?'

Father explained Snapper's plan to record the cosmic truths and Snapper gave a snort of disbelief. 'What else did I do? Flatten the boy's spider with a chestnut pan?' Failing to notice Father's mournful look, he roared with hilarity.

When Snapper shot a peaceful dove from an awning we knew he had recovered, but each of us harboured a strange and secret concern. Snap's brain was a wasteland shunned by its owner. Could such a hulking grotesque change fundamentally for even a moment? It's said god blathers profundities to village idiots — Snap may have gained temporary access to these higher levels of incompetence during the fugue state. Though we rarely discussed it, we were all gung-ho for new information — the present circumstance was a lesson in that it first required us to confess we never got any. This took a rare courage.

Adrienne bit into a stick of celery. 'I'm for knocking him senseless,' she vouched, crunching, 'till he has another fit and spills the beans. If he knows anything of use we'll be sandboys — if not we'll be as pig ignorant as before.'

Father climbed into the treehouse, where Snapper was inspecting the discarded skeleton of a fly. 'I think I speak for us all when I say we'd like to know just what the hell you think you've been doing these last few days.'

'I've told you brother,' spat Snap, whacking the fly with a mallet. 'Can't remember.'

'But brother,' said Father, looking with distaste at a fossilised starfruit. 'What happened to you was a once-in-a-lifetime experience, like being shot and falling from a wrought-iron balcony. Did you find nothing here? No note or message?'

'All I found was a hopelessly blurred photograph of a sobbing clown.'

It seemed the truth had been lost like a poodle in a riptide. 'So you've been amusing yourself at our expense,' said Father. 'To salvage anything of worth we'll have to retrace your sinister footsteps from that moment to this. Now I'm getting out of here — these conversations have been fatal to sturdier men.'

The meandering trail led toward the village, the entire household following the thoughtful Snapper through a wake of smashed lobsters. Father pointed to a stile. 'Ring any bells?'

'I remember standing here and shouting "Watch it!" to a passing merchant before punching his teeth out.'

'Good, good. Anything else?'

'Over the hill there, I seem to recall delivering a flying roundhouse kick to the head of a docile gran.'

'Is that all?' Father fumed.

'Attached a slow-worm to my ear and entered the village.

Bought a corduroy otter in the corner shop.'

'And what were you thinking about?'

'Same as ever. Elves and ash.'

'Elves and?'

'Ash,' repeated Snapper.

The finch of perplexity perched on Father's sill.

In the village Snapper showed us where he had loaded up a diecast crossbow pistol. It was all coming back to him, he said. 'Sprang out pronouncing a scream. Shouts of alarm. Pell mell. Clueless. Knife. Gore. And that's when the fighting started.' He pointed to a frazzled strand of kelp, laughing uncontrollably. 'I stood there bellowing like a cyclops. Had the presence of mind to keep my arms parallel with Mercury's declination in the sky and ...'

The signs were not good. Every stupid thing he did involved physical violence and yelling. We were prejudiced enough to think this could not result in wisdom even when initiated by the individual. And the prejudice was bang on target — the only real impact was caused by a complicated accident we could scarcely believe, involving an angry swan, a first league reserve team and an exploding main. Snapper ended up running through the village with his hair on fire. 'Knew from books that I should try to extinguish the blaze,' he said with a muscular pride. 'And it wasn't difficult. Dipped my head in somebody's sink, and asked them to fill the basin with water. That was that, you see?'

'But you've hardly *got* any hair, you demented old sod,' Adrienne remarked with an uncharacteristic vehemence.

Watching Snapper, I could see a realisation stir like a waking mummy. 'That's what *I* was thinking,' Snapper gasped, and dashed into a barn. 'In there,' he said, pointing at a haystack. It seemed his baptism of fire had borne something by which we could profit after all.

Three hours later, haggard and covered in straw, we found a ragged note which a startled graphologist would subsequently verify as the work of a pig with a snout like a railway buffer. Upon initial examination we could only frown.

'Is this *it*??!' shrieked Leap, appalled, and threw it down so that he was free to grip his own face and weep at deafening volume.

'It's as I thought,' muttered Father. 'You can be sure you've won an argument when the idiot you're arguing with announces he has.' He showed me the note:

Life is a chessboard with one piece and one square. I was born bald and bald I'll be again. That's me. Snapper.

FATHER SON

Father looked up from the paper. 'Thank your lucky stars you weren't born a manatee, laughing boy. Every one of those blighters has been torn to shreds by a boat propeller. Nobody cares over there. Doped to the eyewhites, driving boats, laughing. Damn them all.'

'Weren't manatee mistaken for freshwater mermaids in the old days, Father?'

'Yes. By explorers so desperate for company they'd lob it into a moray.'

'I suppose what with flubbery lips, desperate sailors and lacerating outboards, the manatee are the most unfortunate mammals on this dry-run-for-hell you call the Earth.'

'Not by a mile, child. Because there was once a gentleman entitled August Strindberg whose works were deemed the fuel of the future. "Print another book, Strindberg," his friends would snigger, "the fire's going down." Subtle wits struck him in the face when they realised what he had to say. But this was as nothing to the fact that wherever he went and whatever he did, he was forever being attacked by dogs. The events of his life were

—117—

indelibly interwoven with the snarling and unaccountable umbrage of hounds.'

I had unwittingly put Father in a storytelling mood and nothing short of a hard shake from a lion would stop him now. My eye wandered glassily to the drawingboard, on which the Hall plans were spread like an Escher vortex.

'As a time-saving measure he was born in a state of severe depression. No sooner was he an adult than he found himself backing out of halted parties brandishing a scatter-gun. Social embarrassments of every stamp. And the dogs, by god they had it in for him. Ferocious? You don't know the half of it. Some stood on their hind legs and boxed his eyes. Five of them tied his ankle to a piano which they threw into the sea. He once yelled his problems to a monk, who was first offended, then regal, then pointedly absent. Strindberg went home hanging off the back of a speeding tram, kicking at galloping hounds with his free leg. You're old enough to know these things, boy.'

'So when did he get time to scrawl *A Dream Play*?'

'Locked himself in a cellar. Heard the skittering of hounds above him and that's what drove him on. Emerged a year later to his cost. Rammed by a sudden vehicle.'

'Unceremonious?'

'What do you think? One of the first motorised hit-and-runs on record. Car hit him so fast he was knocked momentarily to a standing position before passing out. Bumper'd be worth a bob or two today. So he was barely out of hospital when a bison hurtled into him on a salt flat. Tried to use it as an alibi.'

'Alibi?'

'Done for murder. Just a knifing, nothing grand, but enough to put the childproof on his career. Growing old and free, he contracted a changed nature. Surged straining against one of those stretch-brace back exercisers which he'd tied to the doorhandles of a church — propelled backwards down the aisle during a ceremony, killing a priest and a pious old hag who remains resolutely dead to this day. Went on like that his last three years. Dog statue on his tomb, looking proud.'

'He died?'

'Not often enough.'

'But Father, that's not a story, it's a mess.'

'It's a life. You want order in this world — here's the closest you'll get.' He pointed to the Hall blueprint. 'Nice plan eh, laughing boy? Starts and ends with the reading room. Fractured or a jigsaw — which do you think?'

'It depends how you approach it?'

'Good answer.'

FACE VALUE

In the first three minutes of the universe, a hyper-concentrated dot of matter and energy exploded, space unfurled to accommodate the supercondensing gases and Uncle Burst's ego broke away from the body of creation, expanding at an unimaginable rate. This much has been verified, but after months of gloomy silence at the dinner table Burst tore off his bib and roared in no uncertain terms that he devoted every ounce of his strength to keeping 'these features of mine' on the front of his head. He stated that his face was the first thing to have emerged from Earth's primordial soup, and said he would reproduce the event in a giant flask. This comprehensive outburst halted the meal, Snapper's jaws frozen in the act of closing upon a wren. As we had always predicted, Burst had flipped from his rocker.

Snap surged to his feet. 'You're meddling with nature you bloody fool — look what can happen!' And he pointed at the Verger. I think Snap was eager to divert attention from himself at this time as everyone had started joking about his spring-loaded ribcage. We all knew he spent whole days laying in the woodland undergrowth, male-volent anticipation flushing his face as he waited for someone to step on him. The sarcasm started when a hedgehog blundered across Snapper's belly and Snapper returned to the Hall complaining warily of a sudden gallstone. Leap had once had a gallstone like a meteorite and recognised Snap's reluctance to compare notes for the shame it was. 'I think you'll find there's one less hedgehog snouting through the bracken tonight,' he announced, looking sharply at Snapper.

So when Burst began building a Urey reaction vessel, Snap was scornful and relieved. The vessel contained hydrogen, ammonia, methane, water and hydrogen sulphide — the stuff of life awaiting a spark of electricity. This spark was arced through the vessel at one-second intervals and Burst set up a time-lapse camera to shoot at the same rate. The atmosphere in the flask reproduced that of pre-biological Earth and when the lightning-wire flashed the entire mistake would be recreated in miniature.

We should have known it would be a turbulent event when Burst started muttering 'Stand clear' over and again from dawn till night. The day of the experiment we stood on the landing outside of Burst's room, our features illuminated by the strobing light. The ticking electrode was the only sound until a blazing explosion blew Burst through the door in a litter of fragments.

'Is he alright?' asked Father.

'Only by the broadest definition,' frowned Leap.

Burst was in complete shock, his eyes locked upward in their sockets, eyelids flickering. The room was filled with smoke and the gas flask was utterly annihilated. 'What did he see?' gasped Leap, convinced that Burst's stupor was the result of having witnessed an image which would have stunned a hardy bull. He salvaged the dented camera with a strangled cry.

The next day we gathered to watch the time-lapse footage. Burst was propped among us like a length of timber. Leap portrayed concern and stated that a second viewing of the horrors in the flask would release Burst from his catatonic state. We were all curious, knowing that Burst's facial claim was a real possibility. He had long since established that the lines on his right palm precisely reproduced the impact patterns on the lunar surface. But why should confirmation of his latest theory blaze him into shock? Was it the first time he had seen his own face?

On the screen we saw a flickering downview of the flask, in which steam appeared to swirl and mass. It soon became dense and brown, streaking the flask walls with nucleic acid tar. A dark protein sludge bloomed at the base of the vessel, changing colour rapidly. The rich mud congealed, heaving, and unfurled from the centre. A face emerged like a plastercast from a vat. It was Snapper's. The film ended abruptly.

As the lights went up, Snapper was triumphant. 'Ha, ha, ha — there you go, Burst. It takes a *real* man to be the first carbon-based life form out of the primal matrix.'

The rest of us were stunned and, to my knowledge, Burst never spoke or moved again.

Unable to leave well enough alone, Leap raided Burst's notes. The only related items he found were a drawing of the flask setup, a belligerent account of Burst's emergence from the primordial stew and a scrawled speculation that the carbonised freeze-impression of that event could be found on the crust of a solar satellite. This was years before

I saw the Viking Probe photographs of what appeared to be a giant face on the surface of Mars. This face, too, was unmistakably Snapper's.

BRAINFOLD

'We all have a cage of bone around our heart,' said Adrienne. 'But you take the biscuit. Anyone with enough sense to fill a bird's ear would tell you this is the spice.' She was referring to the enfolded sunny glade of pollen and opening century flowers, surrounded by hedge-doors and a vale of entrances and dripping gardens which riddled into mazes so distant in all directions that the landscape streaked into mist. The pearl-blue sky showed no sign of abating. The ground sat still, covered in grass. Blown-out watches lay around like shells of snails. Adrienne was drowsing, gold mothdust in her hair — scratch her surface and you'd glimpse heaven.

As we lay in the blurcolour and the shade of leaves, I thought of mossy graveyards and forgotten patients. 'You're not angry at me are you?'

'Ofcourse not — what an idea. You worry too much.'

'I worry subject to requirements,' I said. 'This world's about to spring like a steel trap.'

'No it isn't,' she said sleepily. 'I'll keep it open ...'

She was drifting off. I felt cheated — we had set up a

Bigot Hall

shared dream to be together and now she was falling asleep inside it. Could she have another lucid dream inside this one? How much dreamtime could she cram in this way, like the layers of a Russian doll? I felt excluded, and stood, storming off through an arched topiary doorway.

Slowing away down a hedgepath of crimson litterleaves, I thought about the moon and how any emotion there had to be imported. I watched corrosive gushes furnacing in the sky and thought of skulls tumbling like popcorn. I thought of unsuccessfully killed fence wood growing again. I thought of the skeletons of angels. I thought of giant bonsai. And that people should dream in many ways or one dream would sterilise the world.

Around a corner was a marble bench with an inscription on the backrest: 'We live in an infinitely untidy universe.' I sat down and, finding the seat refreshingly cool in the close heat, I recalled a poem of Adrienne's:

> A beggar sat on a marble bench
> And bit off the head of a dead, raw tench;
> A bigot sat on a marble bench
> And bit off the head of a whippet.

The trees hushed in a breeze. Chuckling fondly, I remembered when I was younger and me and Billy Verlag played with marbles golden as the molecules of lions.

I awoke with a start. I was in the hot-house, on a chair. The glass was blurred with condensation. Infuriated that I'd popped out of the dream — and was now two dream layers away from Adrienne — I bounded up and stormed out. 'Living myself down to their level,' I snarled aloud as I crossed the empty courtyard. 'Hello?'

The house seemed deserted. Some of the windows were open. Everything seemed real enough. The detailing on the walls remained the same when I looked away and back again. I flipped through a book, reading and rereading certain sentences. They never altered, but what did this prove? For some time now I had been accurately transcribing reams of phantom text.

In tutoring me in the lucid arts Adrienne had surprised me by stating that in the last ditch a practitioner may indeed pinch himself to determine whether he is dreaming or awake. I had thought it amusing that we gauge our presence in the world by the ability to suffer. Toying with the idea of using other people's pain as a gauge I had kneed Snapper in the face during a particularly nightmarish conversation, accomplishing nothing but my own entertainment.

Now here I was in the Hall without even an uncle to strike. I pinched myself on the arm. Felt a twinge which may have been a mere recollection. Sat in the quiet kitchen, I punched myself in the face. Terrible face-ache, some blood, but it seemed such a strange, dreamlike thing to do. I hammered a nail through my hand. I smashed my head through a sheet of glass. I slashed my wrists with a bolt cutter. I smiled my throat with a circular saw. I painted the wall behind me with a level-action shotgun. I unravelled my intestines like a bog roll. Sheer agony all of it, but I wasn't convinced. I sat listlessly sorting a duodenum which gleamed like porcelain. Clearly I should be dead by now, or at least unconscious. Everything was reversed. Emotional pain is the stuff of real life as there's no blackout point. This was surely a dream. The kitchen resembled an abattoir.

Then Adrienne entered, stared in utter shock, walked unsteadily to the table and sat down as though medicated.

'Laughing boy,' she said. 'Why such a loss of blood?'

A loud explosion went off in what was left of my ears. 'Are you saying this is real?' I demanded aghast, shaking a ribbon of gut.

'Oh, laugher,' she said mournfully.

'It's a shrieking nightmare,' I gasped, surveying the gore.

'Yes,' said Adrienne. 'You haven't woken up. You fell asleep inside the dream, like I did — you followed me. This is a replica of the Hall where I go to be alone.'

I saw the full horror of what I'd done. 'I'm really sorry, Adrienne,' I said, replacing my spaghetti-like innards. 'I didn't mean to intrude. You're not angry at me are you?'

Adrienne stood, reached over, and slapped me so hard I woke up on the marble bench, the heavy purr of bumble bees thrumming the air. I stood and walked down the hedgelined path to the sunny clearing, where Adrienne stood waiting. She tenderly pushed the fringe from my eyes, then slapped me so hard I awoke in bed.

It was dark, rain was hammering the windows amid low grumbling thunder.

The door opened quietly and Adrienne padded in, squirming in under the covers. 'It's cold,' she said and softly stroked my cheek. 'Your poor face.'

'Are we awake now?'

She made the same tilted, listening expression she made when cutting her own hair. 'Yes,' she concluded. 'Let's not fight again, laughing boy. Look how much time we've wasted.' She showed me the bedside clock. We had been asleep nearly two minutes.

MANDIBLE

New arrivals at the Hall were a cause of excitement and concern and this was never more apparent than the day we were joined by Mr Mandible, who sat in Father's study like a principled man.

'You were referred to me by Roger Lang,' said Father. 'What can you say to redeem yourself?'

'I would like a room here.'

'You and a million others. How old are you Mr Mandible?'

'Thirty-four.'

'Correct. Do you heal quickly?'

'In a flash. Unless the wound is open, as with a triangular chunk-blade.'

'Or a tubular coral injury,' suggested Father, 'sustained off the Hawaiian islands.'

'Precisely.'

'I should tell you that the meals here are acutely poisonous.'

'I intend to grow cress on the mantelpiece and pretend to be happier than I am.'

'Excellent. This all seems to be in order.' Father regarded an action shot of Mr Mandible booting a terrier off a cliff. 'You understand that the ground floor of the west wing is crawling with nuns?'

'This won't be a problem.'

'And that my mother-in-law is made of metamorphic rock?'

'That, with all due respect, is not my concern.'

'Well answered.' Father held out a hand. 'And welcome aboard sir. I think you'll find our little nation a fertile chaos of throbbing trash.'

'Indeed sir,' said the new arrival, with a firm and solemn handshake.

An hour later, Snapper burst into the study. 'Leap's just told me you accepted a new lodger!' He was startled and alarmed. 'Who is he?'

'Strap-hanger. Plug-ugly. Armed to the nines. Ask no questions. Last resort.'

'Is he suitable?'

'I sat here blathering the worst sort of nonsense and he never clanged an eyelid. Shook my whole arm like a man of honour. He'll be up in his room now, buggering a rayfish.'

'Perhaps,' said Snapper, shuffling and eager to begin, 'I should go and give him the glad hand.'

Father returned to his drawingboard. 'See that you do.'

Snapper entered Mandible's room and Mandible, about to flip the catch on his travel case, did not smile. 'Not interrupting anything,' Snapper told him. 'Thought I'd drop by to welcome you into the fold. You'll find this a pleasant home if you keep your depravities to yourself. That hole over there is for the snake, so keep it clear. The corners of the house are all on the inside. Designed to leach your integrity as you sleep. Madness moves upon us with hardly the snapping of a twig.' Snapper sat bouncing onto the bed, looking around. 'This was my room before my brother — who incidentally likes to eat human flesh — told me to live in that treehouse out there.' He regarded Mandible, awaiting a response. 'So how do you make a living, Mandible?'

'I'm in the brain trade.'

Snapper stood and departed with a slam.

In the study, Snapper slavered a substance resembling guacamole. 'Said he was in the brain trade. The *brain trade*,' he emphasised. 'In god's name make a remark to *comfort* me, brother.'

'Perhaps he was lying.'

'If that was the lie he selected what pit of hell could he be *concealing*? You've picked a spooky one there, brother. He'll trundle in at night and suck out your supper with a pipe and bellows.'

In the afternoon, Mr Mandible slowly entered the study to find Father alone at his desk. 'I should like,' he stated, 'to take the opportunity to explain a certain remark at which your brother was perhaps disconcerted. Before matters become unnecessarily oppressive.'

'Oppressive,' said Father, cautiously.

Mr Mandible sat down opposite the desk. 'In the likelihood that you will implore my assistance shortly in the extermination of certain vermin, I have with me the instruments of my calling.' He patted the shell-shaped leather case on his lap. 'You see, what you perhaps blithely refer to, through the cigar smoke and laughter of after-dinner conversation, as the human brain, is not by nature an ingredient of the human organism. The brain is a parasitic sea-sponge, brimming and sinister, wielding our bodies like a crane.'

'A parasite.'

'You mock my trade by pretending otherwise. More things in heaven and earth sir.'

'I should say so.'

'And these particular things,' stated Mandible, 'exist at my expense — and yours. Who needs a forebrain?'

'Ah — who indeed?' said Father, gripping his chair as though in a runaway sidecar.

'Insidious sir. Threading through the host tissue. Staked to the brainpan like a hiking tent. The man who realises all this will feel a strong urge to lance his own head like a boil. Resist sir. Or to cop it under a skidding lorry. Resist, resist. It is not impossible to lead a normal life.'

'An interesting concept.'

'Corruption sir. Pollution. How to discern between our thoughts and theirs? Do I slap my face — uh — by my own volition? It's a sad day for one and all when a man can't take credit for slapping his own profile. And all because of these bloody sea animals.'

'How do these tiresome brains of yours move inland?'

'Tortoises sir. Sold commercially. Thick protective shell, ideal cavity size, slow gait unlikely to jolt the cargo.'

'A skullcase on legs eh?' said Father thoughtfully, standing. 'Pardon me a moment will you?'

Father was in the driveway, frantically loading tortoises into the jeep. He pulled away in a spray of gravel as Mr Mandible ran out of the house, aiming a customised harpoon gun.

Near the village, Father threw himself into a callbox and dialled, gasping. 'Roger you bastard?' he bellowed down the phone. 'Mandible. Seemed normal. Tipped his hand. Madman. What are you going to do about it?'

'Me, old fellow?' laughed Roger Lang affably, his voice crackling and distant. 'He's no friend of mine. Staggered out of an abattoir during demolition. Bothered me. Gave him your address.'

'Well he's fallen just short of invoking the devil.'

'Not surprised, old man — coals to Newcastle.'

'My reading of the situation is this — you're a shithead who ought to be posted a burning rag. This extraordinary admission of yours to not even know the man makes everything crystal clear. He was barely in the door before launching into a dismal regatta of barbarity and fear. Insisted that tortoises contain brains.'

'But ofcourse they do old fellow.'

'Not that kind of brain you idiot. The kind that comes out of the sea and takes control.'

Lang was feeble with laughter as Father dropped the receiver and bolted from the callbox — Mr Mandible was fast approaching on a bicycle. The car wouldn't start — Father started sprinting across an adjoining field, holding a carpetbag.

For reasons I refuse to understand, most of the villagers had come to believe that the Hall was an asylum. Seeing this as his trump card, Father entered the village police station and put the carpetbag on the counter. 'This bag,' he gasped. 'Full of tortoises. See for yourself. Chap just escaped from the Hall. Irrational behaviour. Believes they're related.'

The officer on duty peered into the bag. 'Perhaps they are,' he said.

'Not the tortoises you moron,' shouted Father. 'The facts.'

The church bell began to ring and Father ran out to see that Mr Mandible was clinging to the steeple, yelling down at a gathering crowd. 'Listen to me — don't deceive yourselves,' he was shrieking emphatically. 'We're prawns in their game — you don't know what you're up against. Only one life to lead and frankly you've made a balls of it. We're heading for a catastrophe you fools — a cataclysm from which nothing fiercer than a chicken will step away. It'll be as much fun as being sawn out of a Volvo and as interesting to watch as Walter Brennan. You're in denial, the lot of you.'

Gazing up, the police officer gave a scornful snort. 'Not me,' he said.

'You soppy bastards,' Mr Mandible was bellowing. 'More noisy than efficient. Hamfisted and bleating. Mean-spirited. Imperilling everything. I draw no distinctions. You'll end up as charcoal statues. Baked to perfection. Blown to bits. Revenge. One in the face for liberty. I'm incredible, stunning, unbelievable. And I've been that way for donkey's years.'

The policeman raised a megaphone. 'Had a bump on the old noggin eh Mandible?'

'I'm past caring,' yelled Mr Mandible. 'I've the lion's share. I'm laughing. Your lies are dense enough to fluoresce in UV light.'

'As delirium goes,' said an onlooker, 'it's classy.'

'Makes it look so easy,' said another.

'Mutant in a belltower,' said a third, wistful and misty-eyed.

At that point it began to rain and the crowd dispersed. The officer left, saying 'It's all yours, doc' to Father as he gave him the megaphone.

'Er ...' said Father through a squeal of electrical feedback.

Huge drops of rain were flying from Mandible's face and hair. He sputtered and frowned, clinging to the steeple.

'Er ... Mandible.'

Mandible strained his face around. 'What *now*?'

'You may not be suited to the Hall after all.'

'You ... you said I could stay. There are the legal aspects to consider. A spoken agreement is technically binding.'

'I ... I know it is, Mandible, but ... I feel I've been misled. This brain business, it won't do — not when it involves harpooning tortoises and so on.'

'You didn't tell me,' shouted Mandible over his shoulder, slipping and clutching at the roof.

'It's a house rule, Mandible — one I felt didn't need spelling out. My mistake old fellow, but there it is. No harpooning of anything smaller than a barn.'

'And Mr Burst's ego?' said Mandible, his face pressed against the streaming tiles.

'An exception — all egos an exception. Is it agreed?'

'No turbot,' shouted Mandible.

'If you insist, old boy. Do we have an understanding?'

Mandible scrabbled for a handhold. 'Very well,' he said, and slipped, crashing through the roof of a horsebox — a gelding burst through the doors and galloped away with a confused Mandible on its back. A week later he was found convulsing in a disused sty and by that time Father had organised a course of tablets — the same medication, incidentally, that Uncle Snap took for his anger. In order to keep track of the Hall tortoises, Mr Mandible devised a pair of heat-sensitive goggles which he wore twenty-four hours a day. And since tortoises are cold-blooded and undetectable by these means, the device was a comfort to Mandible even when one was crawling across his face.

RISE

Glad of the company of a gormless tyke to whom he could feed outrageous bullshit, poor Mr Cannon would spin me the same yarn every time he had a break from maximum security. 'You're descended from werewolves,' he said, going at his leg irons with a bandsaw. 'Why d'you think Uncle Snap's forever howling at the moon?'

'Because he's a throwback and barking mad.'

He eyed me with sharp good humour. 'Why d'you say — "barking"?'

I explained that if the lifespan of the world was a twenty-four hour clock, humans would appear at two seconds to midnight and Snapper appear at teatime.

'Precisely,' said Cannon. 'And aren't you always saying he's only just learnt to walk on his hind legs?'

'It's a metaphor, Cannon — something a strumpet like you wouldn't understand. Don't drill here, you moron — take it to the foundry.'

'Think carefully, laughing boy — haven't you an appetite? If it so much as moves you pour milk on and eat it.'

'Out of sheer bloody desperation!'

'No smoke without fire.'

'You know very well there is — get out you bastard and take your ribboned premise with you!'

'Don't say I didn't warn you,' he said, standing up with a smirk of mischief, 'turn thirteen and you'll know exactly what you are.'

But after three years of being drip-fed such effervescent nonsense I no longer bothered to reject it. Amid the unnameable abjections of the Hall it made a refreshing change from the truth and was quietly absorbed into the charcoal of my flash-fried personality. I had always known the others were keeping some grand secret from me — Mister Hieronymus had said as much. Clearly I would start roaring at some point and undergo an agonising change, my bones thickening and creaking like the plot of *Uncle Silas*. I'd howl at the murky window and so on. I was glad to have something to look forward to.

Fascinated by the idea, I lay at night believing that I sensed the onset of the transformation. Adrienne became worried that I no longer struggled against my chains. 'It's no fun when you're like this, laughing boy. Won't you pretend for me?'

'These chains are the best idea you ever had, sister. Come my birthday, we'll need them.'

Adrienne pouted so that her mouth, regrettably, resembled the suction pad of an octopus.

'The werewolf,' she later read from a monster encyclopaedia, 'can be killed by a silver bullet through the heart.'

'So can I.'

'There's more. It's covered in hair, eats sheep, sees in black and white and is easily enraged.'

It became clear that we were dealing not with a mythical beast but a vapid adult male. I saw the slow-motion fire-bombing of my spirit. 'Tighten the chains,' I blurted. 'It's a bloke I'm turning into.'

'That's not terrible,' said Adrienne scornfully.

I told her to take a gander at the precedents. Uncle Snapper — nought to sixty in five hours. Roger Lang — oblivious to anyone but himself. Father.

'What about him?'

I slammed into Father's study. 'No hanging and shooting Uncle Snap this birthday, Father — I want answers. Why has poor Mr Cannon been telling me all these bloody years I'm due for the wolfhouse? I've been straining to endure an erupting musculoskeletal system because of his lies.'

'He meant it kindly, lad — a distraction. Misguided ofcourse — you could park a ship in his madness. People make a meal out of a tedious transition. Truth of it is the meatheads you deplore were meatheads from the start. Snap, for instance, thundered antlered and snorting into his teens without a twang — just got louder, is all. Here's a picture of him aged two.' Father showed me a picture of a toddler at the handles of a Gatling gun. 'Same goes for the ineffectual,' he said, becoming balmy and philosophical. 'Whatever the quality, it's expressed to progressively exponential extremes. The power-hungry will inevitably run for leadership and the drab will support them — but you know this, laughing boy.'

'I suppose so,' I frowned, picking up a clock from the mantel. In five minutes I would be thirteen. 'But what'll happen to someone like *me*?'

Father's face froze with fear, then seemed to crumple. 'I could be wrong,' he stammered. 'Exceptions to everything under and over the sun ...'

I couldn't watch his uncertainty. Returning to Adrienne's room, I lay down on the bed. 'Tie me up,' I said.

HAZE

'Remember a chap who played the petal-pulling game with the pin of a grenade. Got as far as "She loves me" and blew to pieces like a dandelion head. That's the way to go, laughing boy.'

'Yes, Father.'

There was a table set out under a tree in front of the house and some of us were examining a meal. The tree had thrown branches in all directions with a vigorous irregularity. Uncle Snap said he could shoot the cloth out from under the tableware. I had to stand up to laugh.

'The Dodger there,' muttered Snap to Father, nodding in my direction. 'I can't stand him.'

This veiled utterance signalled the start of the morning argument. 'Rattling your chains,' rumbled Snapper, 'untroubled by the snares of reality and expecting it all. You and your infantile aggrandisement have buried the rest of us in steaming bullshit.'

'Beg pardon, Uncle?' I asked, turning to him. 'Miles away.' A vein in his temple bulged like an inner tube. 'Don't look at me that way, Uncle — not without pupils.'

Snap turned to Father. 'The boy's beyond everything,' he said, voice shrill with incredulity. 'Feed him poison and he'll grow fat on it, laughing in your face!'

'Fine words,' I stated after a considered silence, 'from a man who has a vestigial tail in the shape of a Cluedo character. Tell it to a court-appointed psychiatrist, Snapper. You contain enough hot air to fire a cob across a ten acre field.'

I knew I was punching him in the head, an activity I have never been able to control — but my thoughts were elsewhere. I pondered the way a manta ray will filter plankton and small fish from water passing over its gill arches. There's efficiency for you.

My attention returned to Snapper. 'That's *another* time he's punched me!' he complained each time I punched him.

'More in sorrow than in anger,' I lied. I was so angry I could barely maintain my own accent.

But I had forgotten the Duel Rule. As teenagers Father and Snap had argued. Father had set fire to the bill of his brother's hat and shoved him through a plate glass window. To settle the rip they had a handgun duel which went wide. This tradition had been preserved like a tequila worm. At thirteen — an age I had never thought to see — I was ripe for the consequences of my belligerence.

I'd done it now. As the day grew hotter my hopes of survival turned to mist. Leap was painting a starter mark on the lawn. 'It's about that time,' said Mr Mandible, regarding his watch. 'Thought I'd tell you before the appropriate moment's past — your head, it looks like a spud.'

'Thankyou.'

'Ah, don't thank me,' he said and wandered off, cheerful and vague.

Snapper climbed down from his treehouse dressed in combat gear and a ninja hood. Ignoring me, he began a preparatory breathing exercise. 'Laughing boy,' said Leap, startling me — I spun to face him. 'A word in your bell-like. Your lethargy has wrought the havoc we are used to. Even the flowers have ceased functioning as a result of your leering hatred. You've contributed more than anyone to the hellish incineration of human understanding. I feel a raw bleeding wonder when I see you lacking expression from ear to ear. I'd split my own meat to know what you're up to. Watch your back.'

'Better get over there, laughing boy,' said Father, striding up.

'I seem not to have any choice in the matter,' I said morosely.

'The darkest hour's just before the dawn.'

'So are the majority of bed deaths, Father.'

'You a man or a mouse?'

'I appear to be allowed the understanding of the latter.'

'Well your Mother, Nan, Adrienne and I, we're all right behind you — isn't that right — ? Ah they're talking to Snap. Well, off you go.'

'Au revoir.'

'Indeed — and the best of British luck to you.'

'Then it's goodbye.'

I started across the heat-blurred lawn toward the sentry figures of Snap and the Verger. I felt as if I was walking to the circus and clung to the hope of a sudden, distracting haemorrhage. Everything felt obscenely real as I reached the starter mark. 'Your damnation's on the cards, laughing boy,' stated the Verger, opening the gun box to reveal two machine pistols. Snap took his and slapped in a magazine, braying with laughter. My mouth was too dry to tell the Verger what I thought of him, my mind too ripped to think it. I took the other gun, which was as heavy as a crowbar, and pushed in a magazine uncertainly. The Verger placed the box aside. 'Thirty paces and no pausing to poison the well — agreed?'

Snapper nodded formally. I licked my lips and said thickly, 'You have my sacred word for it.'

'Your sacred word,' said the Verger in disgust. He turned and walked away.

'This monkey's gone to heaven, laughing boy,' whispered Snapper. 'Time to snog god in the eye.'

'I daresay.'

I was quite prepared to lie expiring in a bloodpuddle the shape of the British Isles, slick with acceptance. Goodbye to a world of re-run conversation and louts who swear blind that sand is yellow.

A way off, everyone stood blank-faced and shimmering in the rising heat. Adrienne was wearing the slave bracelet I had given her. Life rammed me between the eyes.

The Verger raised a signal cloth. Snap and I stood back to back, and at the drop of the cloth we were off.

It was just like a stroll in the garden, except that I was about to die. Details were blazing up pell mell. There were useless golden bees and other hilarious insects. Cornflower skies over burnt lawns, bleaching bones and the whiskers of flowers. Copper leaves surrounded trees like happy, fairy-tale blood. The fathomless lake floated like a mirage. The shed was a bronzed pagoda brimming with smug, infuriating sages. The sun was dripping like an ingot. I saw the sap sweating from a tree, heard the tickle of every leaf upon every other leaf.

Preoccupied with these sensations, I collided with an ornamental concrete leper. Realising my situation, I wheeled about. Snap was in position with a raised gun. This was it. But my mind was still off the hook. I didn't feel worried.

He fired wide.

Who was I trying to fool? I felt such a damburst of relief I started singing discordant gibberish and eating grass and soil, sobbing with hilarity as I strutted like an untried matador. I heard distant applause from the onlookers. The gun lay forgotten nearby, full of blanks. Father would explain that firing wide was part of the tradition — as was being scared shitless.

I knelt on the lawn, peacefully chewing grass and earth. Immense fluxes of heat were rippling the air. The Hall was blurring and warping like a pious motive.

The following day was chilly and damp. The Hall continued to warp.

ONCE UPON A TIME

Near the end I became more fractious about the family, and thought Mr Mandible would understand. 'Most youngsters are provided with memories of fun and alienation, and what do I get — nuns drilling sheetmetal, a dead old woman, a squad of interchangeable uncles and a synthetic Verger. What will I be like when I reach my prime?'

'A master chef?'

'What? I'd rather be glimpsed in a wood now and again, running the other way.'

'A feral enigma, you mean? Really laughing boy, I'm surprised at you. This place seems to me a child's garden of terror and experience, full of sinister flowers and gobbets of pulsating gas.'

'Precisely.'

Mandible began to describe his own life in polychrome terms. 'Certain lack of family,' he said. 'Died all at once early on. At the theatre.'

'How many were involved?'

'Five in all. Large chandelier flattened them, ridden down upon the audience by an unclothed gentleman. I'm told they never knew a thing — though anyone who met them in life could hardly have failed to notice that.'

'They felt no pain?'

'Apparently not. In fact from what I hear of the play I suspect all five of them were dead before the incident occurred. So from then on I had to get by on charm alone, a course of action which culminated in my wrestling an enraged chimp on a rattling bobsled. My endeavours to enlist in the armed forces having been thwarted by my inability to be found, I took a series of blithely unsecured loans until my very eyelids were seized for nonpayment. I had always had a fondness for brains and offal — but particularly brains. Look at that,' he said, gesturing at a murky fishtank and its bubbling cargo. 'A mere four pounder but able to recall the Brandenburg Concertos before you can say Jack Robinson. And all this I owe to my upbringing. The point is, laughing boy, we all draw something from our environment, like soft flesh from bone.'

I gazed around his room. On the mantel was a 22-calibre pocket gun which he claimed reminded him of 'younger and happier days'. A variety of hen jaws were hung on a pegboard on the wall — I was momentarily disconcerted to see that some possessed incisors. 'Do you mean to say this distorted household could serve as a nutrient-rich support matrix for my prowess in every worthy area?'

'I mean simply that you shouldn't blame the slobbering miscreants of this place for behaviour they were exhibiting when you were still bloodshot and unborn. Forgiveness, child, not exploitation.'

There was a thought — and not before time. The Hall was a sanctuary from the fatal banality of a world unable to discern between a boy who's boring and a boy who's bored. My cup was overflowing — but with what?

'So didn't you and your family ever have disagreements, Mr Mandible?'

'Certainly we did.' He picked up a black and white portrait of his parents and peers, smiling fondly. 'My father.' He chuckled in remembrance. 'I once picked him up by the ears and told him to stick his scholarly incomprehension up his arse. God I was unpleasant. Couldn't have been more than three years old. He was angry as hell ofcourse, tied me to a metal cutting lathe. Escaped and snuck up behind him, announcing my liberty with a hydraulic jack.' Mandible had begun to shudder, flecks of foam hailing from his mouth. 'And I told him plainly, "Ha, ha, ha — I don't give a damn!" And I struck him, and struck him — until he knew!'

He grabbed an egg-timer off a shelf and said it contained his parents' ashes, turning it this way and that to watch the flow amid belting laughter. I became bored and left, but was thoughtful amid a germinating insight. That which must be grown out of may rarely be a way of life, and that which is a way of life may rarely be grown out of — both rarities are infinitely precious. Back there was a man with an appreciation of the finer things. I too would have a family portrait — it would be a way of confirming that I was grateful, that their memory was not to be discarded, that I knew there was more to my family than the use I could make of them and that we were sophisticated enough to hang other things on our wall besides esoteric cow-heads encrusted with cement.

So I got everyone together near the hot-house, grouping them like normal people. Even the Verger threw back his hood. I ducked under the cloth of an old tripod box camera and hit the button. In the developing room, it all grew clear. Pointed skyward were the gormless gape, brittle sockets and marbled cartilage the careful philosopher would have expected. I recognised nobody — only the stance and clothing marked them out. On top of every neck was a cartoonish fish head, sucked of flesh and jelly as though in a single gulp.

WHITE SPACE

Despite everything it never entered my head that I should brace myself. 'Laughing boy,' Father once said in the garden. 'Something I've meant to say since you were no more than a comma. See this blade of grass?' I thought he was going to reveal that this was my real father. 'I agree with it absolutely. Man accepts diversity at every level of nature but his own mind. A million emotions; only two hundred words. This is becoming no place for us.'

He was perfectly placid. It made me think of a dream I had had one morning. 'Listen to me,' Adrienne had said while untying me. 'One day you may have the Hall to yourself. It's time to show you everything.' And she pushed at a false wall, revealing a reflection of the Hall without people. I awoke and was still bound to the bed, Adrienne asleep on top of me.

Then there was a conversation I witnessed through a crack after Snap had thoughtlessly stapled my ear to the floor over Father's study. 'Leap was in the reading room,' Father was saying. 'Wrong time of night. Took two books, back to back. Scrambled the text by shaking them like an unopened Christmas present. *Alice in Wonderland* and *Pilgrim's Progress*. Look at this mess: "As I was beginning to get very tired of this world, I lighted on a certain place, and as I slept I dreamed I saw a White Rabbit clothed with rags, and saw him reading a book with a lamentable cry, saying 'What shall I do without pictures or conversations?' " '

'What's the rest like?' asked Uncle Snapper, smoking a cigar.

'Pure hell.' Father threw aside a thick, messy book of jumbled design. 'And it couldn't have happened before. House is losing form. As a folly it's not entirely controlled.'

'That explains the skull bulging out of the kitchen door. Started off as a bubble in the paint, remember?'

'One of the upper rooms has gone — and so has the space it used to occupy. Electric snow. Lucky no one was in there.'

'Everything's going to seed,' said Snapper. 'Including our brains.'

'Only one way to restore the structure. Go through and lock it — those of us who are ready.'

'The boy's not ripe.'

'Hieronymus will provide a warning.'

'And poor Mr Cannon?'

'Pray they find an empty cell.'

Snapper was more relaxed than I'd ever seen him. 'I can't believe I allowed myself to get mixed up in all this.' He gestured with the cigar at his family, home and country of origin.

It should have been obvious. For years Father had been relating his theory of literary transcendence. He said when a person was written into a book that person existed partly in the world and partly in the book, like a body lying halfway through a door. Surely it was possible to pull the body all the way through? He had been saying this since I was young enough to believe there were angels in the fridge. On the reading room shelf was a book with blank pages.

So one afternoon I was sweeping viscera from the orchard when I looked up to see Mister Hieronymus standing in the landscape. 'Who rises from prayer a better man,' it rumbled, 'has forgotten something.'

'What was that?' I shouted, but the figure was gone. I put it down to lurking, pure and simple.

Then I was struck by the weather above the Hall. A bright land under dark sky. A sundial stood at the orchard edge with the inscription 'I count only the hours that are serene'. The dial shadow was bobbing and rippling like a flame. Clouds began to funnel over the Hall. Magisterial distortions warped the air as I approached the building. Little green keys were turning on bushes as growing leaves squirmed. The gargoyles were silent. At the instant I reached the door, the Hall held its breath like an ejecting pilot.

I opened the door onto a maelstrom. Furniture was tumbling through the air and colliding amid white flaying winds. The clawfoot tub in the hallway cracked, releasing coilpiles of garter snakes — each of whom I knew by name — across the floor. Ramone the moose-head was a leer-jawed skull, beyond feeding. I waded through snakes to the staircase, wondering for the first and last time if there might be advantages to city life. As I passed them the bannisters grew into the ceiling like needles into flesh. I could hear the building's central mechanism thrumming like an elevator. Behind the glass door of the grandmother clock the pendulum swung through slow liquid. The glass shattered outwards, spuming seawater. Every door on the landing was rattling — I surged past them toward the Hall's heart. Wood splinters and hectic rain spiralled in the air. Curtains flogged at the walls like the capes of sorcerers. Corners of the house were overlapping with a kind of heaven.

The reading room door was flying open and closed. With each flap the light poured out, streaking through my head with the speed of an idea. The room was like the inside of a daylight bulb. Slamming inside, I stood in an atmosphere torrid with human sparks. Books and paper blurflapped across the circular room, rushing up the chimney. Whole shelves lit up like neon and faded to ash, blowing away. Fluxes of intertextuality pinned me to the wall. There was one shelf left and finally a single book. Swirling fireflies came to a point and fired a ribbon of lightning into the empty volume.

The storm immediately abated. I hadn't any skin. Even my DNA was bruised. I felt as heavy as kerosene. In a shadowy corner lay a book, like an overripe apple. I went slowly over and picked it up. The blank volume had been filled with words. The tone was toxic and casual. The title was *Bigot Hall*.

The Hall was empty. I checked out the foundry, finding the furnace full of clinkers and white powder. An abandoned ignition drill leaned against the battery press. You never know what you've got till it's gone — even the headache I had suffered unknowingly since the moment of my birth now abruptly disappeared.

It wasn't the same without the sudden shots and incoherent yelling. I sat for hours waiting. I sat at Father's drawingboard waiting for someone to rebuke me. I lay in

Adrienne's bed clutching a manacle, shackling myself accidentally and cursing in the quiet house. I leafed through the book, reading about the others and becoming obsessed with the white spaces. I felt certain I should fill them. My every move and thought was precarious. I was halfway there, like a body lying halfway through a door. They were calling like sanity.

There ended the happiest and most conventional phase of my life.

An independent publishing house, Serif publishes a wide
range of international fiction and non-fiction.

If you would like to receive a copy of our current catalogue,
please write to:

Serif
47 Strahan Road
London E3 5DA

or

1489 Lincoln Avenue
St Paul
MN 55105

also published by Serif

THE CRIME STUDIO

Steve Aylett

Brute Parker ran the all-night gun shop on the corner of Dive and Ride, and it was a valuable service he offered. Anyone needing a gun fast at three in the morning ran round to Parker's store to view the extensive range. But nobody ever haggled with Brute Parker whose philosophy was, 'Well whatever it was, it's dead now.'

Beerlight, the city of all our futures, is not a safe place. Crime — occasionally sophisticated, normally violent, always hilarious in its unintended effects — is the motor of the city's economy. Weaponry, rather than fast cars or designer clothes, is the ultimate status symbol. The populace is dedicated to law-breaking, politically incorrect views and hurling abuse and hand grenades at each other. The cast of hoodlums includes burglar extraordinaire Billy Panacea, Kicker Charlie the casino-owner, conman-cum-lawyer Harpoon Specter, Henry Blince the donut-obsessed chief of police, Gerty Hundred Ram the unwitting bank-robber and other fun-loving felons who hang out at the Delayed Reaction Bar on Valentine Street reading the *Parole Violators Bugle*.

A deranged descendant of both William Burroughs and Damon Runyon, the book's narrator is referred to only as 'the clown' by his fellow criminals. Like all wise jesters, he holds up a mirror to our world.

Steve Aylett, recently incarcerated for the attempted robbery of Richard Nixon's tomb, was born dangerously close to the edge of a cliff — but not close enough.

paperback

FAT SKELETONS

Ursule Molinaro

Mara is a translator. In her Greenwich Village apartment she successfully renders her native Czech into best-selling English, until one fine night she notices alarming similarities between her own Prague childhood and a 'brilliant novel' by a rising young star of Czech literature. Making contact with the author, she realises that he had become the protégé, perhaps the lover, of her now dead novelist-mother. She threatens to reveal his plagiarism of her own past and her mother's papers and is soon caught up in a cycle of threats and counter-threats. As the layers of deception in the lives of Mara, her mother and the young author are steadily revealed, the boundaries between literary creation and lived experience begin to evaporate ...

'Wickedly playful ... Molinaro touches her everyday deceptions with the stuff of fairytale' *The Observer*

'A delight ... made me laugh uproariously'
Financial Times, Books of the Year

'A great deal of witty fun' *Publishers' Weekly*

Ursule Molinaro lives in New York City. A writer and translator (of Herman Hesse, Christa Wolf, Philippe Sollers, Nathalie Sarraute, Dino Buzzati and others), she is author of ten novels including *Positions with White Roses* and *The New Moon with the Old Moon in Her Arms* as well as a number of highly-acclaimed short-story collections.

paperback

also published by Serif

THE FOLLY

Ivan Vladislavić

*A less steadfast man might have taken to his heels, but Malgas
stood firm. He even had the presence of mind not to confront the
apparition directly. He sensed danger: he saw himself turned to
stone ... He watched the floating balustrade out of the corner of his
eye. It shimmered, and shimmied, and emitted a halo of brilliant
light. It faded, and was on the point of vanishing altogether, but,
as Malgas's heart skipped a beat, it glowed again with a new
intensity, and appeared to stabilize and solidify somewhat. It grew
a landing, it excreted a film of crimson linoleum, it oozed wax.
Then it gave birth to a flight of stairs ...*

A vacant patch of South African veld next to the comfortable,
complacent Malgas household has been taken over by a
mysterious, eccentric figure with 'a plan'. Fashioning his tools
out of recycled rubbish, the stranger enlists Malgas's help in
clearing the land and planning his mansion. Slowly but
inevitably, the stranger's charm and the novel's richly
inventive language draw Malgas into 'the plan' and he sees,
feels and moves into the new building. Then, just as remor-
selessly, all that seemed solid begins to melt back into air ...

'In the tradition of Elias Canetti, a *tour de force* of the
imagination' ANDRÉ BRINK

'A rare new talent' *New Statesman*

Ivan Vladislavić was born in Pretoria in 1957. Formerly
assistant editor of *Staffrider*, South Africa's leading
independent literary and cultural journal, he lives in
Johannesburg. His first book, *Missing Persons*, a collection
of short stories, won the 1991 Olive Schreiner Prize while
The Folly, his first novel, won the 1994 CNA Award.

paperback